Praise for Insomnia

'Aamer Hussein is a master calligrapher, weaving delicately together the story-shaped ways we embrace loss, memory and intensities of place. His steady, intricate gaze is global, taking war and wounded politics as background to individual experience in Asia or England, from Javan uplands to South Kensington, Karachi to the shaggy coastal paths above 1930s' Folkestone. These profound, beautiful and very different stories illuminate each other, exploring how a generous sensibility responds to the world and other people, especially those who touch us through their own writing. We are, say these haunting stories, a shadow theatre with live puppets, a motif in someone else's tapestry.'

Ruth Padel

'Aamer Hussein's stories of lovers, poets, artists, and thinkers are written with glorious fluidity and great precision. His characters are at home in a world of ambivalent exile; they are reluctant migrants who find kinship and solace in unexpected places. Wonderfully evocative and readable.'

Kate Pullinger

Aamer Hussein

Insomnia

TELEGRAM
London   San Francisco   Beirut

ISBN 10: 1-84659-024-8
ISBN 13: 978-1-84659-024-5

copyright © Aamer Hussein 2007

This edition published 2007 by Telegram Books

A full CIP record for this book is available from the British Library
A full CIP record for this book is available from the Library of Congress

Manufactured in Lebanon

TELEGRAM
26 Westbourne Grove, London W2 5RH
825 Page Street, Suite 203, Berkeley, California 94710
Tabet Building, Mneimneh Street, Hamra, Beirut
www.telegrambooks.com

Contents

Acknowledgments

Earlier versions of 'Hibiscus Days' and 'Nine Postcards from Sanlucar ...' have appeared in *Wasafiri*. 'Insomnia' was first published in *Moving Worlds*. A slightly shorter version of 'The Crane Girl' was published as 'Tsuru' in the anthology *Leave to Stay* (Picador). I'd like to express my thanks to the editors of these publications.

Special thanks in London to Mai, Mimi and Hanan, as always; to Geri for Sanlucar and so much more; in Delhi, to Gagan for Amrita Sher-Gil and Sunday *dosas* and exchanges about insomnia, and Rana, for midnight drives and conversations.

And wherever they might be at a given moment, to my family, without whom ...

I'd also like to thank the team at Telegram, especially Anna and Becky. And to all the other friends in London and elsewhere – you know who you are – who travelled along with me on the highroads and detours of writing these fictions.

Finally, some writers who inspired me: in Delhi last December, I reread the poems of Majaz, who found his way into a story. In Delhi, too, I discovered the writings of Anis Kidwai through a conversation with Qurratulain Hyder; Kidwai's distinctive style as an essayist, and her narration of Partition's events, along with Saliha Abid Husain's writings in many genres, brought me closer to understanding Muslim intellectual life in the years leading to Partition. And, never far from me when I wrote 'The Angelic Disposition', the influence of my maternal great-uncle Rafi Ajmeri (1903–1936), who shares his first name, the grace of his style and the plots of some of his stories with the hero of my fiction.

Aamer Hussein
London, May 2007

Nine Postcards from
Sanlucar de Barrameda

1

Before breakfast, I walked back to last night's perfumed bush. It wasn't fragrant now: I must have smelt a night flower. We breakfasted beneath an orange tree. By the Alcazar gate a chamber orchestra played the Habanera from Carmen. Only oranges and songs to take away.

We are leaving Sevilla. The bus station is crowded, proletarian. My companion wants water, a ham roll, the Ladies' loo. I fear we won't board on time.

A skirmish for seats, but they're numbered. We leave on schedule: midday on an August Tuesday.

2

On board, a confusing text on my companion's mobile. We try to calm each other: aren't we expected in Sanlucar? Is there some misunderstanding? Dun landscapes from the window.

The journey's shorter than expected. God, the vagaries of making electronic contact. My irritation makes my travelling companion laugh out loud.

I stole the term 'companion' from Pavese. In real life friends are all that matter, but 'friend' in a narration sounds coy.

Perhaps we laugh together.

3

My Spanish sister – I call her that, she calls me *hermanito* – is waiting at the little station. We have come to her for her birthday. She drives us to her new house: full of light as homes should be, with airy windows.

A year ago she painted me, in oils. I'm dressed in blue and larger than life, sitting by a window of her London flat. Behind me there's a red brick wall. She complained of London's changing autumn light. Here she paints in her eyrie, in a tower. Her studio overlooks tall palms, jasmine bushes, bright flowers.

Later, with green figs, white peaches, local cheese, we drink summer wine. My sister calls it Poor Man's Sangria.

4

Satiated, seated by the blue pool now, hot as heaven. Anxieties disperse, join red petals scattered round on stone and grass. Birds dip their beak in the pool's water. In the sun's blaze the leaves on their branches shine white. Now I think of the garden I once called home.

Shirtless, I lie on short grass. Its texture tickles my back. My companion, swimming, leaves me to my lonely thinking. (Once we shared summer ruminations. At times our silences run parallel. At others we're like strangers who don't meet.)

The cuckoo calls three times, as brazen as a rooster. Perhaps the sun estranges thoughts, reminds me of advancing age, grey hair, dull flesh. Still, in dreams, I fly before I fall.

5

My sister, dressed in green, is dancing the Sevillana as we enter. Two friends are with her; one dances too, the other sounds the beat with flattened palms.

Sunlight dapples my sister's cheekbones, flickers on her fine drawn features. She dances with her face.

I'd love to paint her like this, in her green flamenco dress, dancing. If I could paint. But she could paint herself. *Tres morenas de Jaen, Axa, Fatma, y Maryen* ... I think of Lorca's songs.

What does *duende* really mean?' Someone asked my sister, at a London supper.

'*Duende* means talent,' she responded. 'It's not a word we use much any more.'

Tomorrow is her birthday. Her grandchildren are on holiday on another continent. My sister, my companion remarks, looks twenty when she dances.

6

Later, on the beach. Pavese called the sea a field. Tonight it is, a silver field.

The sky reddens, darkens, scatters stars.

We're at the mouth of the Guadalquivir, my neighbour says. The Arabs called it something like *wad-el-kabir*.

'Andalusian hospitality, too, is Arab,' someone says.

But this is not the sea. The yellow strand is not a beach. I'll stick to my terms. Sea or river, the line of water remains a silver field.

7

We eat water-creatures: anchovies and anemones, cockles, langoustines and bream. My neighbour speaks to me of ragged love and separation. My mind and tongue unlock their Spanish. We are, at fifty, childless. My companion, eleven years younger, has a son.

'You should have a child, the two of you,' my neighbour says.

'Ah,' I tell her, 'but we're not lovers.'

'We're best friends,' my companion adds.

'Do you still feel Pakistani?' The Venezuelan to my left asks me.

'I do, when I feel anything at all.'

The Venezuelan drones on.

'Muslims in Europe are a demographic problem. In Andalucia, I hear, they want to reclaim ancient sacred places. They should be loyal to their country of adoption. Wouldn't you say?'

'I guess I'm a Muslim in Europe too,' I say. 'And foreign everywhere I go.'

With one desultory gesture I dismiss an uncongenial conversation.

'I'm tired of romance,' I overhear my companion saying.

'But without love life's an uphill climb,' my sister muses.

Now, as I drink manzanilla, I see you in my glass. Perhaps I haven't thought of you as yet, left you behind with other things in London. Finger dipped in ink of manzanilla, I bring you into being from your place of absence, think of writing you into this narrative. (Like me, I remember, you can't swim.) Why do we see yesterday as shadow, tell me, call memory a haunting? Echoed crooked smiles, linked fingers, can thrill, become a sudden presence. Should I write: sometimes I think of you and wonder if you really happened, on occasion wish you were here to taste the green figs and the summer wine – or remind you of an evening's words that spiralled from life's work into euphoria, an empty bottle's cork I kept at dawn, some other things you left behind?

8

At midnight we sit on the patio. My sister smokes a cigarillo, I sip brandy poured on ice. A little lizard, startled, runs up the wall. The smell I remember from Sevilla fills the air, from a bush behind my left elbow.

'Jasmine,' my sister says.

(I must remember this, to tell you: there's no frangipani here, that makes it less like Karachi.)

Now it's nearly 2. My companion has retired to her room, her separate thoughts. (She wanted to visit the Alhambra. Short of time, we couldn't make it.)

Too often I treat friends like lovers, lovers as friends, give children the attention owed to adults. But friendship's all that matters. I have no time left for love. (One night – November, and the moon was full – you told me we had nowhere left to go. For a while I'd dreamed that we might travel on. It doesn't matter any more.)

My sister knows all this. I need to tell her nothing. We sit alone together. The sky hangs dark and low. We continue to talk, of small, of necessary things.

The frangipani tree I planted will be in full flower the next time you're here ... my sister breaks her sentence. Her eyes are very blue.

9

Eyes shut, I breathe in, lost colours found again: jasmine white, fig green, hibiscus red and something new, unnamed: purple, perhaps.

The fan hums overhead. I recall one mad night's crossing, and a morning salutation: parted lips brush mine four times, and then – an afterthought? – a fifth. How should I name so accidental an exchange: inconsequence, or parting gift? What would you say?

Next door, my companion turns the tap on. What, I wonder, woke her? By my pillow, in a vase beside a jug of sparkling spring water, a twig of orange bougainvillea leans on jasmine. Like yesterday, it has no shadow and no smell.

The Crane Girl

1

When they first became friends in early autumn, Tsuru disapproved of Murad's companions, Jime from the Côte D'Ivoire and Vida from Ghana. Tsuru wondered what an Asian could have in common with someone from Africa: was it merely dark skin? She didn't even pause to think about the differences between a Japanese and a Pakistani.

But after meeting Tsuru, Murad hardly had time for anyone or anything else, even his studies; in late November, before the end of term, Mrs Fogg-Martin had phoned his father to complain he'd missed two of her afternoon poetry classes.

As often as he could, Murad would go back with Tsuru to the flat she shared with an Australian girl called Pam and a Canadian boy named François. Sometimes they'd sit in the communal sitting room and listen to Tsuru's collection of American, English and Spanish records. But Tsuru thought that her flatmates were scroungers; she couldn't stand their marijuana joints and the cheap Rioja they loved drinking, and transferred her record player to her bedroom. Murad learned to smoke with Tsuru: or rather, to be able to smoke with her, he taught himself to inhale in his own room, choking, spluttering fumes out of his open window towards the empty patch of land people said was the burial ground of the Tyburn martyrs. Soon he was buying a packet of Players' every day – the cheapest he could find – and telling his father the price of sandwiches in the canteen had gone up.

The tutorial college they attended was in a shady residential street just off Gloucester Road. Tsuru lived within walking distance, in Airlie Gardens; Murad lived off Marble Arch, and he soon discovered he could save fifteen pence a day by taking the bus, which cost less than the tube from Park Lane to Cromwell Road. In the afternoon he'd get off just past Hyde Park Corner and walk home through the park; that was even cheaper, and it helped him save for the cigarettes he bought to replace those he'd accepted from Tsuru and her friends.

When he'd arrived in London in May with his sister to join their father, the park had been, along with the library and Selfridges, their main field of entertainment. There were regular rock concerts – Mungo Jerry, the Kinks, and once the hallowed Rolling Stones. Mahalia Jackson sang gospel unaccompanied and her voice hung over the park like a rainbow. There was also the spectacle of hippies smoking hash and making love in the grass, and Hare Krishna people who handed out lentils and rice to passers-by. In those days they'd had no friends, and films, which they'd seen all the time when they were younger, were expensive unless you sat in the front row near the screen. They went to see Bombay movies once or twice a month at first, possessed by a nostalgia that was almost entirely imaginary, since they'd always had a preference for Western films at home. Passing through the dingy suburbs that seemed to make up most of London filled them with genuine pangs of homesickness for the leafy lanes and elaborate gardens of the neighbourhood they'd left behind in Karachi, or made them miss the broad, airy avenues of the district they'd lived in for three years in Rome. Then his sister had gone to her fashionable girls' boarding school in Norfolk and he, to save time, had been sent to Elliott House to rush through the O levels he'd already prepared for in Pakistan.

Most of the boys in Murad's school were Greeks, Arabs and Iranians, and older than he was: they drank, gabbled away loudly in their own languages, and chased after girls in pubs. Many of his schoolmates didn't wash enough because they thought it girlish to shower more than twice a week, or their landladies simply wouldn't allow them to. Each group seemed to identify with a national or regional label, playing roles written for them by some invisible scriptwriter. There were Malaysian Chinese boys and girls who banded together; Hong Kong Chinese who only had time for their books; and East African Asians who patronised Pakistanis because they considered them backward and insufficiently Westernised. So he made friends with the Africans who had fluent English and open minds.

In the evenings he would stop by at the local library on South Audley Street. Then, unless his father was taking him out to dinner with acquaintances who had offspring he was expected to befriend, he'd usually stay at home with a book, or very often watch exotic films with titles like *Ashes and Diamonds* or *Yang Kuifei* on late-night television. He was developing an interest in Japan through the films he'd seen and a handful of novels he found in translation at the library – he was particularly taken with one called *The Sailor Who Fell from Grace with the Sea*.

When Tsuru came back to school from holiday he was struck by her elegance, which reminded him of the ivory beauties he'd read about, though she didn't strike him as beautiful at first because she seemed so fragile. She usually dressed in black and her hair was ear-length. She had a nearly perfect oval face; her skin was like smoked cream, her eyes were long, narrow and fringed with blade-sharp lashes, her full mouth parted to display very white and slightly protruding teeth. She sat down at the desk next to his, but they hardly spoke until one afternoon when, without knowing why he was doing what he did, he followed her out of the school building after the literature class to the row of shops on Marloes Road. She was going to buy cigarettes. He lingered under a low tree till she emerged from the tobacconists', then fell into step with her for a block before asking her if she'd like a cup of coffee at the nearby Wimpy Bar on High Street Kensington. She smiled, unsurprised, and said yes. They talked a little, mostly about classes. Then Tsuru told him she was nearly eighteen, and had lived alone in London since her father, a JAL employee, had been posted back to Tokyo two years ago. Murad, who'd turned fifteen the spring before, told her how his mother had stayed back in Karachi and planned to join them in London the next year. When they finished exchanging life histories it was nearly 5.30. Murad reached into his pocket for money to settle the bill and found he only had five pence, and it would cost him half of that to get to Hyde Park Corner. He couldn't even pay for his own coffee, let alone Tsuru's. But almost as if she hadn't noticed, Tsuru said, 'You can buy me one next time,' and put twelve pence on the plate. That was her way: she'd pay for him quite thoughtless once, and another time let him treat her or even ask for a loan.

Later, she told him his blush had given away his discomfort: his blush was one of the many things about him that made him the butt of her jokes and teasing. 'Remember,' she loved reminding him in company, 'the first time you ever took me out for coffee you wanted to know if I was a virgin, and then you didn't have money to pay for our coffees? I knew you'd be a bad date right away then.' Murad couldn't remember whether this was true, or one of the many funny stories Tsuru liked to tell about him in front of others. He knew he had asked her about her love life, but thought they'd known each other at least a month by then. What he remembered was the way she'd repeated the word 'virgin', pronouncing it 'baaar-jin', though her English was usually unaccented. And he also remembered her answer: she'd 'played around' with a cousin when she was twelve, and then had had two boyfriends, one who was much older, and the one she was still seeing, Rick, who lived with his parents in Sevenoaks where she often spent weekends. He was bemused, too, by the thought that she'd assumed he wanted to ask her out on a date.

Murad himself had come very close to losing his virginity with a childhood friend during a wedding celebration in Karachi, at which about ten teenagers had turned a late-night revel into a slumber party. But he and his putative sweetheart hadn't really known how to go beyond deep kisses and long embraces; then, as they were fumbling with buttons and bindings, they'd been interrupted by people getting up for drinks of water and visits to the loo. In the morning they were still technically virgins. By the time he'd been in London a few months, he thought it best to be honest, at least to Tsuru, about his inexperience. Anyway, he'd never met anyone remotely suitable. You had at least to like someone a lot to make love with them – and he, where would he meet that someone who'd like a being as awkward and plain as he felt he was?

Tsuru thought his innocence was quite funny and announced it to Pam and François in his presence as soon as she could. 'The little darling, shouldn't be a problem with his looks, he's a nice looking bloke,' Pam hooted. Murad felt his ears and cheeks heat up. 'He's OK if you like dark types,' Tsuru mused, as if Murad weren't there. 'Me, I like blondes.' The word came out as 'bronders', Murad noticed, wondering why Tsuru's accent sometimes betrayed her. But he was aware then, for the first time, that it mattered to him what Tsuru thought about him, and that she shouldn't, as a friend, have made fun of him like that in front of Pam.

2

Once upon a time, in a far-off land, a poor weaver saved a crane from a trap. Then a beautiful woman turned up at his door and said, 'I'm your wife.' She wove the finest fabrics for him, which he sold at a profit. She made him swear he'd never open the door of the room she wove in while she was working. One day he did, though, and he saw a naked crane weaving cloth with feathers plucked from her breast. She flew away then, and never came back. The crane-bride's name was Tsuru.

That's where he'd read the name before: in the illustrated *Tales of Old Japan* he'd left behind in Karachi.

3

Last summer, the summer after the spring he arrived in London, the weather had been bright and fresh, and he'd had to rush out to buy T-shirts and cotton trousers because the clothes his mother had had made for him to take to London were warm, tweedy and quite conservative.

Leaves fell in autumn and he hardly noticed the trees' stripped branches because he spent most afternoons with Tsuru, listening to James Taylor, Carole King, Cat Stevens and Melanie in her room. Just as he hadn't noticed that his hair, once short, then trendily layered, now fell to his shoulders, because his father hadn't been nagging at him to visit the barber.

Then winter brought a blanket of snow for Christmas and Murad was lonely, lonely. His sister had come home for a day or two when the holidays began, and then gone off to spend the best part of the festive season at a farmhouse her new best friend Helena's family owned, deep in Dorset. Tsuru was staying in Sevenoaks over Christmas with her boyfriend and he hadn't made any new friends. But on Boxing Day François and Pam rang his bell. His surprise was faintly tinged with pleasure – he hadn't even known they knew where he lived. They were going to the park: would he come with them? In Hyde Park the Serpentine was glassy. They pelted each other with snowballs beneath the evergreens and rubbed snow on each other's faces. He had never been in snow before, never even seen snow before coming here to London.

He'd always assumed, without really thinking about it, that Pam and François were together, but the way they teased each other about crushes and the feelings of isolation they seemed to share and complain about threw him in doubt. He promised he'd ring them in a day or so, but, in spite of his loneliness, didn't after all – what, apart from Tsuru, did they have in common with him?

He'd done his O levels by then, and started studying for his As. Because school was closed till the second week of January he'd taken to going to study at Kensington Central Library, which had a large reading room upstairs. Much of the time, though, he read novels – James Baldwin, Muriel Spark, Mary Renault and Yukio Mishima were his present favourites. But the true reason for his trips was that Airlie Gardens was just nearby and he hoped he'd bump into Tsuru, who'd never answered any of the telephone messages he'd left with François.

When he ran into François in the reading room for the second time in a week, the Canadian boy asked him back to the Airlie Gardens flat for a drink. He said yes only because it was Tsuru's place, though he knew by now Tsuru hadn't come back after Christmas: 'Not even to pick up her things,' Pam whined. 'She still owes two months' rent, and she's locked her room, the cow.' The sitting room was large, dun-carpeted and on the first floor. A dim bulb disguised its grubbiness. There was a fire burning, 'You've got a friend' played on the turntable, and Murad was surprised by the ease he felt with these people who, a month or two ago, he wouldn't even have considered his friends. And the warmth seeping through him, particularly after he'd sipped the first glass of red wine he'd ever tasted, owed nothing to the thought of Tsuru. In fact Tsuru had a way of making everyone revolve around her tastes, her wishes, her peeves. She'd made him see these friendly, lonely foreigners through her eyes, because something had made her turn away from them ...

He looked at them: slight blond François dressed in denim jeans and matching jacket even in winter, smoking one of his perennial soggy joints, and Pam with her thick green jumper sliding off one plump creamy shoulder to reveal the upper curve of a breast. He'd always thought she was big – if not actually fat – before, but tonight, without the striking contrast of Tsuru's slight presence, the sturdy body and lush curves seemed quite attractive. They look like a lady and her suitor in some old Dutch painting, he thought: the lighting and fire are just right, though the clothes are all wrong.

'And she kept trying to turn François against me, because she can't stand having any boy paying attention to another girl,' Pam was saying, her eyes as narrow and green as a cat's beneath her frizzy red fringe. Murad had been daydreaming and didn't know what had led to yet another Tsuru story, but Tsuru was what he, François and Pam had in common. And people did like to talk about her. He'd noticed that even at school classmates would pass remarks about her as soon as she left the room. 'You know, she walked into the bathroom one night in her bra and panties while François was showering; she'd had a fight with Rick. She just stood there and looked at him. François told her to get out ...'

'Shut up, Pam,' François began, but a half-instant too late. Murad had already said, 'I don't think we ought to be slagging off Tsuru when she isn't here, at least she says what she thinks in front of us all.'

'Well, she said you were morose and childish and she spent time with you because you were so lonely – always following her around.'

Murad knew his face, already flushed in the artificial heat of the fire, was turning an even deeper red, that familiar blush again, and he was filled with mixed reactions: the pounding sensation in his forehead he identified as anger, the melting wax in his entrails was guilt. Here I am, he mused, sitting in this room I know only through Tsuru, listening to her music on her turntable, and enjoying her absence. But I don't believe she'd say such things about me.

He stood up to leave, but a conciliatory François was brandishing the wine bottle with one hand and tugging at his arm with the other, pulling him down to the cushion he'd been sitting on. Soon Pam was pouring even more wine into his tumbler and the semblance of cheer was about to return. At least they've got each other, he thought, they seem to do everything in harmony and be such good friends. And once again that lonely feeling he was so familiar with since Tsuru and he had said their abrupt telephone goodbyes before Christmas invaded him. Pam's tales had made him, if only for a moment, doubt Tsuru, the only real friend he'd made since he arrived in London.

On Saturday evening he was back in the Airlie Gardens flat, surrounded by people dancing, lounging, smoking, accompanied by the strains, passionate and plangent, of a Santana album. He couldn't imagine how Pam and François had crowded about sixty people into their sitting room, and wondered who they all were: they both complained they hadn't many friends. He was dancing slow, cheek against Pam's warm cheek. He, François and Pam had gone to an afternoon show the day before, and when Pam had excused herself to go to the 'little girls' room', François had whispered: 'She really likes you, you know', and when she came to sit next to him he moved slightly closer. But before he could work out what to do next, she had his hand in hers and was licking and biting the knuckles of his fingers. Suddenly his fingers had found themselves in her blouse, circling a nipple, and her hand was reaching up his denimed thigh. The feeling that had started as a curious little furry animal when he had looked at Pam lounging by the fire the other evening was turning into something slyer and more predatory, a wolf cub gnawing at his lower belly. So now he knew why he was here. He'd told his father he was going to spend the night at François', without mentioning Pam.

Pam was about five feet nine, and François probably five-eight, but Murad was over five-eleven, very nearly six. Pam could rest her head on his shoulder as they danced.

Murad awoke at 5. Pam was snoring quietly beside him. He didn't have a key and he knew he shouldn't ring the doorbell before 8;

his father would wonder why he'd left François' place so early on a Sunday. He had a bad taste in his mouth after the half-bottle of cheap red he'd swilled again without liking it, and no memory of pleasure at all – only the feeling that if this grappling and wrestling was what everyone wanted him to learn about, well, then, he'd learned it all quite easily and it was no big deal, just a slightly messy and uncomfortable collision of muscle and bone. And the heaviness of someone's body against his, sweating even in the chill January weather, had made him shrink to the edge of the bed at the risk of losing his part of the coarse red blanket. All last night's attraction had completely gone in the grey dawn light that seeped through the half-curtained window.

He rose from the bed, showered and washed till his winter-sallowed skin was red, dressed quietly in the bathroom and went into the sitting room where one figure, wrapped in a blanket, lay on the sofa. He thought of going into the kitchen to make some coffee. He knew where everything was, he'd often brewed drinks for himself and Tsuru to take to her room. But then he thought better of disturbing the sleeper. He hovered for a moment – he didn't want to go back to Pam's bed, because he felt guilty again about what he'd done, sleeping with a girl he wasn't remotely in love with.

Then he heard François' unmistakable Quebecois tones: 'What's up, man? Up so early? Can't sleep?' François lurched naked out of bed, draped his thin cream blanket around himself like a toga, and stumbled into the kitchen. 'Coffee.' It was more a statement than a question. He come out with two steaming mugs, handing Murad one stamped with the welcoming motto of some seaside town and embellished with a handle in the form of the head and torso of a hideous woman with protruding breasts.

'How did it go? Did you make it?' he asked, and the thought came to him: François does share her room. Her bed. I knew and didn't want to know. She threw him out so I could stay over with her. Suddenly he felt better, because if he'd used Pam she'd used him too. And then he felt worse: no, it was a game Pam and François had played, it didn't matter to them really, in some odd way they were using him to get back at Tsuru.

'She really fancies you, you know,' François muttered, reaching for some Rizla paper and a lump of the dope he loved smoking. For a moment, Murad wondered whether he meant Pam or Tsuru. And Murad saw that François, for all his streetwise ways, was probably no older than he was, maybe even younger, and he didn't understand the games Pam was playing, though he thought he did. And under the world-weary mask he was hurting.

Pam telephoned three times over the next two days. He spoke to her the third time because she'd called at 7.45 in the morning, and her persistence was wearing out his father's nerves. Murad arranged to meet her in the park at 9, and walked with her to a bench near the Serpentine. He'd splurged on a pack of Dunhills for the occasion. Lighting two, he handed Pam one, struck a brooding attitude, and said: 'You're a sweet, lovely girl, Pam. But it isn't going to work, you know. We're just light years apart.' He'd heard Richard Burton say something like that to Elizabeth Taylor on a beach in a film he'd watched on television late one night.

'It's that bitch Tsuru, isn't it? It was her you wanted all the time. You made a fool of me. Pig. You were thinking of her when you were with me. She slept with François, you know, even while she was with Rick. That's what she's like, she'll take on anyone if she's in the mood. Bloody scrubber. I'm surprised you haven't tried.'

Murad knew his mouth was hanging open and, for the first time since he was seven, his eyes were about to water.

'And you know what else? I bet her a bottle of wine to a Santana album that I'd have you in bed before she did. She said you'd never look at me. Ha, ha, ha I say. And ha ha ha again.'

'I don't believe you,' Murad said. 'You're lying. You're muck.' He turned on the balls of his feet. Hoping she couldn't see how he was trembling with the effort to control anger and tears, he strode off through the park without saying goodbye or looking back.

4

Missing Tsuru was now such a habit he'd almost stopped noticing how much he still did miss her. She'd become an image of everything he didn't have – companionship, affection, adventure. He hadn't tried to contact François even though he

31

felt sorry for him, since there was no neutral ground for them to meet on. But François, too, seemed to have disappeared along with Pam.

Murad had signed up for English, French and History this year. A level classes were held in a bigger building – further away from home, in Brook Green, which meant a longer journey there and back. Though his bus route took him past it every day, and past the Wimpy where he'd first sat with Tsuru and got to know her, he avoided using the Kensington library, because he just didn't want to see François: it would probably embarrass both of them too much.

He had new acquaintances, a handful of Pakistanis, Indians and Malaysians with whom he had coffee and cigarettes at school and occasionally met outside. He even had a new best friend. Shigeo wasn't in any of his classes, but they seemed to have the same lunch break on Tuesday and to leave classes at the same time on Thursdays, so when one day they found themselves walking towards the bus stop together and then getting on the 73 bus, they started talking. Shigeo was dark-skinned for a Japanese; he had long, straight hair, parted in the centre, which grew down to his shoulders, and a faint birthmark on one cheek.

'I'm getting off here,' he said as the bus passed the Albert monument and approached Exhibition Road. 'Would you like to visit?'

Murad just smiled and followed him off the bus.

Shigeo brought up Tsuru almost immediately. She'd lived

with her father in the same block as Shigeo before he went back to Japan.

'Miss Shimomura's very strange for a Japanese girl. Maybe because her mother's half-European,' Shigeo said over a cup of tea in his narrow bedroom. He was squatting on the floor while Murad sat on his bed. Then, probably in response to Murad's quizzical expression, he added: 'Goes her own way. She's free. She borrows things. Money. She goes out with too many boys. She's noisy.'

How many boys adds up to too many may be a matter of perspective, but one boy in all the time I've known her, if you discount Pam's lie about François, is hardly many from any angle – and she's hardly noisy, Murad thought. Then he recollected how once, after she left a room, he'd felt that she did, in fact, take over in a group, even in her silences, projecting a restlessness by sighing or running fingers through her soft hair. She also had a way of stringing together her sentences with gasps, sighs, digressions and subordinate clauses, so that even a simple story became a bravura performance. She could be an excellent listener, though, when there weren't too many others around.

'I didn't know you knew her that well,' he said aloud.

'Not so well ... she asked me to keep some of her records for her when she was moving out of the building. She left behind a lot of strange records,' Shigeo told him. 'She still hasn't picked up some of them, but I hardly ever listen to them, don't understand the music she likes: wailing and screeching.'

As if to illustrate his point, he took the Janis Joplin album *Pearl* from a rack and in an almost defiant gesture, slung it on the turntable. The Bourbon-scented notes of 'Take a little piece of my heart' filled the room, but Shigeo kept talking, about music now. His passion was Western instrumental music, and he'd studied violin since he was five or six, but had been discouraged by a teacher from training to become a classical musician. He'd switched to the guitar.

Though Murad knew nothing about Western classical music, he felt compelled to ask Shigeo to play something. Shigeo's countenance darkened as he swooped and swayed over his Spanish guitar, his fingers rapid on the strings. He played two pieces, one of which had a vaguely Moorish feel. Then he stopped, wiped the perspiration off his forehead with a towel, and announced: 'I'm going to play something different, now.' The melody he played was simple, five notes repeated in different combinations, now playful, now melancholy. From time to time he'd pluck at a string with two fingers. Murad was put in mind of water falling on leaves, and then of wind whispering to water, and then, again, there were echoes of some strange bird's song. It couldn't have lasted more than five or six minutes, but Murad had closed his eyes and opened them after what seemed like an age. He tried to find something appropriate to say, but only came up with: 'What's it called? Was it Japanese?'

'I made it up,' Shigeo said. 'As I played. Right now. Shall we call it ... Cranes Flying?'

As Murad was leaving, Shigeo picked up a bag, slipped the Janis Joplin album into it, and handed it to him with an incoherent murmur of explanation. He wondered if the reference to cranes had been deliberate, but he didn't know whether the Japanese word for crane was Tsuru, or whether Tsuru was just the name of the crane girl in the fairy tale.

Somehow, people often seemed to assume he had access to Tsuru, or was the guardian of her things.

Sometimes he wondered: was it a growing need for companionship that made him respond to Shigeo's extended hand of friendship? His only real friend until now had been Tsuru and, when she left, Pam and François, who were her friends. Or at least he'd thought they were her friends until they'd proved to be no friends at all; instead of filling in the space she left, they'd only made it blanker. Perhaps the initial response to Shigeo had been because he was, like Tsuru, Japanese. But Murad couldn't think of two personalities so unalike. They didn't even seem to belong to the same world.

With Shigeo the only effort Murad had to make was to go along with his invitations, which were, much of the time, issued as statements. 'Today we'll see *The Music Lovers* at the Kensington Odeon, it's about Tchaikovsky. Today we'll try Indian curry. Very sunny weekend, we'll go to Windsor.' Soon after they met, Shigeo's parents invited Murad out to dinner with his father at a Japanese restaurant where they sat around a low table as if they were kneeling, but actually there was room for them to dangle their legs in the well beneath the table. Murad's father reciprocated by calling them to the house, where he served ten people food he'd ordered from a fancy restaurant and had it served by a protégé he'd hired for the evening, an accountancy student who needed extra cash. There wasn't likely to be a great friendship, but, in good Asian fashion, once the parents had eaten together the sons were at liberty to see a lot of each other and even to stay out late on special occasions.

Shigeo bought a car on his eighteenth birthday, and he was willing to buy tickets, make plans, organise, and never seemed short of enough money to pay for two. When once, in passing, Murad mentioned his father had finally promised to take him, at his insistence, to see a production of *Hedda Gabler* with Maggie Smith in the title role, Shigeo sighed and said he'd been wanting to go to that too. Murad's father fell out of the plan as soon as he heard that someone else was willing to replace him, handing over his ticket to Shigeo with his characteristic brand of exasperated generosity. He later remarked that Murad had been accepting too many favours from the older boy and they shouldn't take that, or for that matter each other, so much for granted. After the harrowing performance, to get rid of the gloom that seemed to have overcome them, Murad suggested eating at a pizzeria adored by trendy students – a place he could afford on his pocket money. Shigeo, back in control now after having admitted his wish to do something Murad had wanted to do, said he couldn't stomach cheese and insisted on treating Murad to an expensive burger at a place near the park instead. A renowned rock singer was dining with his entourage at the table next to theirs.

What Murad had once taken as oriental formality – you could hardly, after all, call Shigeo reserved – turned out to be a combination of self-possession and extreme moodiness. Shigeo seemed to know what he wanted from the world and how to go about finding it. He moved around London as if he'd lived there for ever, though he'd only been there a little longer than Murad. At times, Murad wondered what the older boy, so serious and seemingly independent, saw in him; Murad was not a flatterer, and neither of the boys very demonstrative. Shigeo made it quite clear that he didn't want to have anything to do with Murad's school acquaintances. He'd move away politely if he found Murad in a group, or call off abruptly if he rang and Murad mentioned friends were over. Murad made sure to do exactly that – warn him there were people visiting – after Pinky, a girl in his history class, dropped in unannounced once while Shigeo was over at his house, and Shigeo was convinced the visit was prearranged. Shigeo didn't seem to have any friends of his own; when Murad shyly asked him about this, he said: 'Japanese teenagers in London are childish and boring.' Murad felt he'd been intrusive; Shigeo rarely asked personal questions, and it was often hard to remember what they talked about when they parted.

Shigeo could suddenly lapse into very long silences, which often didn't matter while they were at the movies or even immersed in their own thoughts as they walked in the park. Over cups of coffee, though, or sitting in each other's rooms, these silent spells would fall over them. And Murad would think of Tsuru.

When the time came for Shigeo to drop everything and perform a guitar solo, particularly if it was one of those wildly romantic Spanish melodies he favoured or something minor-keyed that seemed to have a Japanese feel, the music would somehow evoke Tsuru, her presences and absences, and he'd think of how she talked and talked about everything like a bird flitting from wire to wire, about travelling and poverty and family wars, and how he had something to say in response, always, even when he felt she'd lived so much more intensely than he had – this daughter of divorced parents, a free mover in a world he'd barely started learning to recognise ...

And then he'd be encouraged to dredge out his own secrets, hurts and fractures and fears half understood, so that even if he couldn't completely express himself or Tsuru responded as if he'd said something disingenuous or naive, he'd be left with feelings to examine and deepen. He'd started writing poetry then, and continued. Much of it came from rather dark dreams he had, or was inspired by music, or by those vague feelings of isolation from the group he sensed Shigeo shared with him. Once, in his room, he'd showed some verses to Shigeo, who'd hemmed, nodded his head, and said: 'Very good English, very good ... mmm ... images, but maybe a liiiitle bit above my head.' He raised both slender hands like a cradle above his head. Murad hadn't made the effort again, though Shigeo often asked him: 'How's the poetry?' as if he were enquiring about an eccentric and slightly unsavoury relative.

One afternoon, when a conversation about something entirely trivial – the relative merits of Western and Eastern music, perhaps, or Ken Russell's style as a film director – was edging quite close to a display of tempers, Murad made an excuse to leave Shigeo, and, walking through the park with a spring drizzle descending, thought the moment had come for them to spend time apart. Murad didn't like asserting his views and tastes the way Shigeo did. (Recently, when trouble had begun between the east and west wings of Pakistan, Shigeo had asked him about the situation as if he wanted to pick a fight, and Murad uncharacteristically retaliated by bringing up Japan's treatment of Korea. But that was a long time ago, Shigeo said, Japan had learned its lesson.) What, after all, did they really have in common, apart from their loneliness? Being foreign boys in London? Their dark hair and eyes? It wasn't as if Murad was planning to drop Shigeo: he'd just avoid him for a while. Their friendship had become too much like a habit.

He didn't answer the phone that weekend. But there weren't any calls except one from Pinky, his Pakistani classmate, who wanted to borrow some history notes. She came over on Sunday; they strolled down the Bayswater Road to look at ethnic bric-a-brac and some terrible amateur art. He stayed home on Tuesday because he had a headache and a very sore throat. But when the doorbell rang at 8 and Shigeo, hair cut unfashionably close to his scalp, stood in the doorway with a heavy Mates bag in his hand saying he'd been late-night shopping and had dropped in to see why Murad hadn't been in for his Eng Lit class, he had to admit he was relieved. Shigeo didn't accept a half-hearted invitation to stay for supper: he left after an hour, a cup of coffee and a cigarette. It was only after he'd gone that it occurred to Murad the shops on Oxford Street stay open late on Thursday evenings, not Tuesdays.

5

On Saturday, Tsuru summoned him from a phone booth on Bayswater Road: 'Meet me in the park!' He slipped a pair of soft moccasins on his bare feet and went to meet her by the Peter Pan statue. Tsuru stood silhouetted against a backdrop of spray from the fountains. Her hair was longer, shoulder length, cut raggedly at the edges; she'd gained a little weight. Her long eyes were edged, unfashionably, with black kohl, and even in May she was dressed in a black polo neck and a long black skirt. She held out her arms and he went to her, bending down to kiss her preferred cheek. 'You've grown taller,' she whispered. 'I feel like a midget.'

They walked across the park to the café on the bridge, to which they'd often come before.

'Where did you go, Tsuru? Where've you been? Not a message, not a postcard ...'

'I went home,' she said. 'To my mother, this time. She sent me a ticket. To Seville, she was visiting Andalusia with her new Viennese husband. I went to Morocco too. And Venice. So grey in spring! Now I'm back at Rick's, but we don't really get on any more, not the way we used to ... you know he just isn't growing up and I treat him like a little brother and that drives him really mad, and his parents just don't relish the tension or even understand what's up between us, so I'm looking for a room in Kensington, to be close to the school again; I'm coming back in autumn. Have you taken Spanish? I want to take up Spanish again and do French and German, too.'

Time passed without his noticing. Every question elicited a detailed answer from both of them. He realised how much he'd been talking, he hadn't talked so much since she left, and he was suddenly embarrassed by the sound of his own voice. He started laughing when she said: 'Hey, calm down, we have time.' Then, leaning over the stone slab that served as a table, he put a hand on her hand and kissed her cheek, nearly spilling her coffee. She blushed and grinned. 'Calm down, shaggy dog. I'm glad I'm back, too.'

That's the way it is with Tsuru, he thought. She knows what I'm feeling without my having to say anything. But he didn't want to talk about François. Or Pam. And she hadn't asked.

Then he remembered. He looked at his watch: 5.55.

'God, I'm supposed to be at Marble Arch. I'm supposed to meet a friend at the Odeon.'

41

'Oh, I was counting on spending a little more time with you. Well, I can catch the 6.25 from Victoria, I suppose. Walk me?'

'I'm late already. The show starts at 6.'

'Stupid of me to think you'd be free to drop everything, even for your old friend who hasn't seen you for a long, long time, on a Saturday evening. Who are you seeing? Anyone I know? Girlfriend, by any chance?'

'Boy, actually. No, you don't know him ... well yes, you do a little. Shigeo Matsubara.'

'Matsubara? That creep with the Spanish guitar? A friend of yours? His father works for JAL, too; I suppose you know he lives in the block we used to be in. Well, he's such a girl, you might as well have chosen a girl instead. You've moved fast while I was away, I must say. Following my tracks, were you? François, Shigeo, and Pam ...'

'Who told you about Pam? That's all a mistake, anyway.'

'That you kept phoning her after I left? Stayed over on New Year's Eve? And went back to Airlie Gardens three times and made passes and pestered her until she'd had enough of you and told François to throw you out?'

François, push me out? he thought. He's more your size than mine.

Lies, lies, he wanted to say. Instead, he blurted out the story about Pam and what she'd said, the backbiting, the bets.

'I? Bet Pam you'd sleep with her? Me? Would I care? Well yes, I would care, I wouldn't expose any friend of mine to such trash.'

(She said 'tulash' in her excitement.)

He'd made her miss her train now, she said; but he could go off to see Matsubara, she'd just wait alone at Victoria Station for the next.

He thought it best to continue with his arrangement. To give her the upper hand now would start him, once again, on that road he'd been on before, of waiting for her calls, bearing her absences, putting up with her snide remarks and sarcasms. 'Look, Tsuru, I'm sorry, I didn't start anything, but if you want me to I'll say I'm sorry, I'm so glad you're back ...'

Tsuru was laughing soundlessly, as she often used to do when he started stumbling over his own words. 'Listen, I almost forgot. Open this. Put it on.' She took out a little box in which nestled an exquisitely crafted watch with a silver strap. 'For your sixteenth birthday. See? Even in Venice I was thinking of you on the day.'

For the second time that day, he leaned over to kiss her cheek. But it was her mouth that met his, warm, moist, slightly open.

6

It was past 10 by the time he got off the Number 16 bus at the Speakers' Corner stop, after seeing Tsuru onto the 9.25 from Victoria. Never having been in a situation like this before with Shigeo or anyone else, he didn't know what he should do. Phone and apologise? Shigeo's father would pick up as he often did in the evenings, and Shigeo would probably refuse to take his call. But when he came to his block of flats he saw Shigeo's car parked in the drive. Shigeo must have seen the film on his own, come out and called, and Dad must have told him I wasn't back yet, Murad thought. Now I'll be in trouble because Dad won't know where I've been, and he'll think I'm lost or that I've been lying about seeing Shigeo.

Shigeo had rolled down the window of the car and, cigarette in hand, was beckoning to him with that palm-downward gesture of extended hand which had disconcerted him when he'd first encountered it – in Pakistan it would be considered quite rude, but it was usual among East Asians. Murad went over, apologies making his lips feel like jelly, but Shigeo merely gestured him into the car. On his breath was the smell of more than one beer.

Murad didn't ask where they were going. Driving through the park towards the Albert Hall, Shigeo told him he'd waited at the cinema till the film began, missed the first few minutes, then phoned from a coinbox when he came out to see where Murad had got to. No one had picked up the phone. He'd phoned again several times. So it was fine, then; Murad didn't have to worry about Dad wondering where he was – Dad was out, and if he came back and didn't find Murad at home he'd assume he was with Shigeo.

'A friend called me,' he said. He thought Shigeo deserved some explanation. 'I thought I'd have a cup of coffee with her in the park and come along to meet you at the Odeon, it wasn't that far away, I could have walked there in a quarter of an hour. Then we got talking, I hadn't seen her in months. It was Tsuru. You probably guessed, anyhow.'

(There was more, so much more, he wanted to say. We walked, hand in hand, to the round pond. The sun hadn't set yet but we could see a pale, full moon. We sat and we talked and we talked but I couldn't tell you what we talked about. I wanted to tell her what I felt about her, what I've probably felt about her since we met, but I couldn't. I started to say something but she put her finger to my lips. I kissed her hand and then I kissed her cheek and then I kissed her mouth. I could feel her eyelashes, brushing my cheek. We got up and we walked to a tree and we lay down under the tree and I held her very, very close. She had her head on my chest and I could smell her hair. It was drizzling now and though I wasn't cold I was trembling and to my surprise she was trembling too. I felt as if nobody had ever touched me before. As if I'd never touched any one person before. I could say much more but I won't. I'll write a poem about it all. About her.)

Shigeo placed a restraining hand on his forearm.

'Let's eat. I'm hungry. Have you eaten yet?'

(Then she looked at my watch and she said: 'It's late. I have to go.' I didn't say anything. I followed her. I took her to the station. She gave me her cheek to kiss as she got on to the train like she always does.)

7

At the All Night Burger place on High Street Ken, Shigeo ordered a lager with his food and drank it quite fast. Murad, who'd sworn off alcohol after the New Year party at Pam's, had ordered a coke because he thought it looked childish to have a milkshake – which was what he really wanted – while Shigeo drank beer. Shigeo toyed with the chips on his plate, left most of his burger, and ordered another lager.

They sat silently over their plates for a while. Murad, who was famished, finished everything on his. Then he asked: 'How was the film?'

'Good. I'll see it again with you. Or maybe you can see it with Tsuru.'

Murad noticed that Shigeo hadn't referred to her, the way he usually did, as Miss Shimomura. He didn't reply. He was used to these silences of theirs, so maybe he'd just have sat there silently and not mentioned the film. But this time he thought, Now I've started this conversation let's get it over with soon, then we can both go home and perhaps I'll write a poem. But Shigeo was still talking.

'Male friends are the only ones you can count on, you know? But as for you, you're in love. It won't last, though. Don't worry. I've been there. I know what it's like. Sorry, maybe I'm talking too much, but I'm drinking, and in Japan we say sometimes you drink just so that you can tell the truth about things. And you're my friend so I think I should talk to you truthfully. I like you. I like you very much.'

He put his hand on Murad's in a gesture that was at once rough and almost a caress, more intimate than any that had ever passed between them. His eyes were dark, slightly bloodshot and very intense. His hair was growing raggedly, and stood out in tufts. Murad let his hand lie beneath his friend's for as long as he possibly could to avoid a movement of withdrawal that might seem abrupt. But when he did take his hand away, to light a cigarette, Shigeo seemed to see it as a sign to resume his monologue.

'I've been where you are now. I've had a girlfriend too. For nearly six months. First we were friends, then we became ... we had so much we shared, background, tastes, language, and we were both foreigners here. We spent all our time together. We became ... close, you know? I'd never been with a girl before in that way. But she had. With one boy, she said, but I began to think there were others.' But she began to change as soon as we'd been together two or three times. Just because we were together in that way, she said, it didn't mean there was anything special between us. She wasn't in love with me. She'd loved her other boyfriend more. I'd get jealous and angry and I wouldn't call her for a day or two and then she'd call and we'd meet and she'd say I was her best friend and that's what she really wanted, a true friend, that's what was really important, and friends could make love too if that's what they both wanted, but if one of them becomes possessive then that's when the problems begin and making love makes everything so much harder ... and I was trying too hard to hold on to her. She couldn't breathe when I did that.

'Earlier she'd felt that I was like the brother she'd never had, a younger brother, though we were about the same age. What she'd liked about me when we met was that I was gentle, soft and gentle like a girl, she said, but now I was acting like all the rest. Like her ex-boyfriend. Like her father, who'd called her mother Eurasian trash and chased her away ...

'I got ill. I don't know what happened, but I was ill for many, many days. She'd come over almost every afternoon after school, sit with me, tell me funny stories about our classmates and Japanese kids we both knew. She'd hold my hand, sing, talk, and I thought we were really together.

'I got better. She didn't ring me. She didn't answer my calls when I rang. Then one day I saw her on the street and she told me she'd moved. She was sharing a flat with some friends in Kensington. They were having a party on Saturday. I would come, wouldn't I? And bring some beer or wine.

'I got there late, because my parents had some visitors. I walked into a dark room. Crowded and smoky. I couldn't make out too much at first, but then, I saw her. She was sitting on a cushion in the window seat with a boy. A blond boy. I recognised him. Her ex-boyfriend. They seemed to be arguing. But they were drinking from the same glass and taking drags of the same cigarette.

'I stayed where I was and if she'd seen me she didn't show any sign of it. Her flatmate came up to ask me if I wanted a drink and

I said yes, followed her to the table where the wine was, filled a plastic glass and moved away. When I got back to where I'd been, they'd gone. I felt there was no point in staying on. My head was spinning, I felt suffocated there, it was summer and really, really hot. I don't know how long I stayed, a half hour? I remember the songs that were playing just before I left the party, 'Lola' by the Kinks and that song about the summertime that was so popular last year. I went onto the street. There was a car parked just outside the door. A two-seater. A couple in it, embracing very tightly. A blond boy and a girl with black hair. They sensed someone standing there and parted. The boy looked down but the girl looked me straight in the eye.

'It was Tsuru.'

8

Somewhere, there's a country where cranes come down and change their form. In a land where there are cherry trees in the shadows of mountains with peaks of snow that never melts. And if you're lucky you'll save a crane from a trap and she'll come to your door and stay with you and spin you fine brocades. But you must never ask her where she comes from. And you must never open the door of that room in which she spins her secrets.

That's what Shigeo did. He opened the door. And Tsuru flew away from him. I don't think he's lying about anything. I don't think he ever even meant to tell me about it and even last night he was trying to keep her name from me but it just slipped out. It can't have been another Tsuru, can it? No. I think the reason he was drawn to me in the first place is that he knew I was close to her. It must have been only a little while after they broke up that she and I became friends. Or perhaps she was still seeing him. But he said it was summer. The summer that, when I got to know her, was nearly over …

Murad stopped writing. He had been trying to study that morning and then, when he couldn't concentrate, he'd made an effort to write those poems about his evening in the park with Tsuru: he'd had them in his head, word-perfect, with some semblance of rhyme. But what he'd written instead were these rambling passages about Shigeo and the story he'd told last night.

Murad had come home very late to find the door latched on the inside. He hadn't dared to ring the bell and wake his father, but he wanted to pee and eventually he had to ring. Gingerly. But his father didn't answer. So he'd had to go down, very timidly pee under a tree in the park, and then ring from the callbox across the road from his block of flats – probably where Shigeo had tried to call from earlier. Dad had an extension on his bedside table and answered after about four rings. He let Murad in and said: 'Enough. No more late nights. I thought you'd had an accident. Your friend had called and said he'd waited for you at the cinema and you hadn't showed up. Then he called again after the film, from across the road. When I said you weren't yet back he said he'd thought you might have come in late and sat somewhere else. He'd looked for you but still hadn't found you. I want you home at 11 at weekends and during the week you're to be back before 8. And you're not going out tomorrow or seeing Shigeo for a week.'

That was fine. He thought Shigeo and he would need to be apart from each other for a while to adjust to the new circumstances. Shigeo had frightened him last night; now, at a distance, he was moved by the older boy's intense declarations, his rough attempts at intimacy, the look in his dark eyes, the slurred parting words and the grip on Murad's forearm as he'd driven him home last night: 'You won't let me down. Please.' But Shigeo, in spite of his warnings, must know that Murad was going to keep right on seeing Tsuru, and he wouldn't like it. How would he react? As usual, with a few days of silence before a reticent overture? Keeping Shigeo and Tsuru in different compartments of his life was going to cost a lot, because, whatever either of them said, Murad needed them both and he didn't want to be forced to choose between them. Unless one of them asked him to. He hoped they never would, because he knew who his choice would have to be.

Tsuru had said she'd come back, next Saturday. He didn't think she'd have found a new place in London, so if his father had cooled down by then he might just ask if Tsuru could use the guest room that night. Or for a few nights. To have her close, breathing and sleeping so near ... and she might, if he didn't press her or persuade her, tell him the whole story. Many stories.

For now, though, he had his own version of her story to write. But he didn't know if it was his or Shigeo's.

It didn't matter.

He turned to a fresh page and wrote: *They say there was once a young man who fell in love with a girl called Tsuru ...*

As he wrote, he heard the wings of birds circling above his head, the sound of running water, and, in the distance, the notes of a guitar, echoed by the call of a flute and the soughing of the wind.

Hibiscus Days:
A Story Found in a Drawer

1

I'm lying on my stomach in Armaan's sitting room, but it's a room I don't recognise. I'm reading a book he threw at me as he passed, on his way to fetch us both a cup of coffee. It's an encyclopaedia, full of pictures of moths and butterflies.

Suddenly, as I wait, I feel the room throb with the music of a hundred miniscule white wings marked in blue. I see them gleam like candles in the muted light. 'Armaan, Armaan,' I call, 'Come and see, the moths from your book have come to life.' But when he comes in they've disintegrated, dissolved into the light.

I told Armaan about the dream – on the phone, before these days of electronic mail. He laughed. Later, at a symposium, I heard him recite a poem in which he'd used the images of my dream. I wanted to tell him he'd stolen my vision. But he'd made it his own.

I filed the incident away in a mental drawer for years. Until two days ago.

I was on the tube on my way to meet a friend and see the postwar Afghan film about the Taliban that everyone was praising. As usual I was sitting with a journal, *The New York Review of Books*, open on my lap. I was hardly reading. An odd white movement distracted me. I looked up: there in the tube compartment at 2 on a Saturday afternoon was one of the blue-painted white moths of my dream. And then I knew that all the work I'd done on Armaan's life was incomplete: I had to begin again, search for a hidden dimension, and open up, in the process, the infernal box of my own pain.

Armaan, my friend, my plagiarist.

Time now to talk about him. A poet with long bony hands and a faint red scar that ran from eye to temple. His name: Armaan Sadiq Hassan.

I could start, I suppose, with his obsessions, contained in the set of fables and poems he sent to me from Karachi in the summer of '86. Samar had seen him on a brief trip to Karachi and he'd given her the parcel of poems for me. We tried to figure out what he wanted to say. Armaan had once held that only politically engaged forms of art made sense in a country like ours. In those early days at university we all sat up nights discussing critical realism and docufiction and the sacrifice of the lyrical urge. Armaan would point out that our best poets – Faiz, for one – had been highly politicised but they hadn't sacrificed one red drop of the lyrical. It's a question, he said, of vision: of finding the right names for things. Recharge the language with your blood.

Armaan wrote in Urdu. He left it to us to translate him into English; I don't know much about the other local languages. With an ironic grimace he'd concede that English occasionally united us Third Worlders. How else would he be understood by a Malay or a Palestinian?

The early work he published was full of pain and political passion – he retained all the intensity, if not the grace, of the poems he'd produced in his college days. Those were about a search for identity and self. But the new lot of texts we were looking at now – hallucinatory images of birds, death, rain, fire, birds, death – seemed to be from a nightmare world that was beyond our comprehension.

Samar said: 'He's given in, or given up. I think the break-up with Aliza's destroying him. She told me when I saw her that he gets morose and drunk and then manic, bangs his head against wall, burns himself with cigarettes. She says he hit her once and didn't remember. He accused her of sleeping with women from her human rights group. He made her abort the child she was carrying. He hasn't even tried to get a job since they threw him out of the paper. He's translating textbooks into Urdu and giving private tuitions. The only hope for him in Karachi is a 9 to 5 job and the private life of a mystic. All-night *qawwalis* and that sort of stuff.'

We agreed, though, that Armaan's delicate wordstrings powerfully captured the claustrophobia, repression and loneliness we'd felt in Pakistan in the early Zia years. Samar and I had been running back and forth, thinking of friends who wanted news and books, but we were always careful not to say too much: we wanted to go home and stay free of the escalating paranoia that grabs the self-important expat by the throat. Not that anyone in Pakistan gave a damn about what insignificant migrants like us were saying in London or New York, but we didn't want to embarrass relatives and connections in places of power.

Samar had a consuming need for Pakistan – I called it an addiction. It was all the more consuming when she was abroad. I'd tell her: 'The craving's more powerful than the cure, longing's your vocation and your profession, it's more important to you than I am.'

2

Now there are three of us. Once there were four. Armaan, Samar and I had been students in England at the same time. There was also Aliza. Those three arrived in the same year. Aliza and Armaan already knew each other – we never worked out how – in Karachi. Samar was from Islamabad, but she'd lived in Karachi as a child. We'd studied together at the American school, which was how we first met. Then I left: my parents were posted abroad for years, and travelled all over Europe. (They were, until recently, in New York, constantly planning to move back to Pakistan when the situation became more stable – they left the States just before September 11 and live in Karachi now, two lanes away from my married sister, in the house they spent years building and then rented to a foreign consul.)

All of us had some remaining links with Karachi. I had my sister, who'd moved back when she married. Armaan had his older half-brother who'd saved up to see him through his education when their parents died. Aliza's feudal-industrialist clan seemed to own half the city.

Aliza came to Cambridge from Columbia, where she'd taken a degree in linguistic philosophy; it was all Saussure and Wittgenstein for years. At a conference she recognised Armaan, who'd arrived in England on a scholarship complete with all the courteous trappings of his lower-middle-class Karachi upbringing. She decided to take over his re-education, but she soon realised she was the one being remade: his marked lack of affluence gave her the street credibility she felt she still lacked. To the onlooker it looked like instant love.

Samar applied for postgraduate studies at Oxford and was accepted. Zia had been in power for a while. Reports from home were bad and she said it was futile for her to go back. I was the least motivated member of our group at the time. I registered at Essex for a doctorate in comparative literature. I specialised in anti-colonial francophone fiction, in which I saw parallels to some pre-Partition Urdu poetry. That led to an underpaid job in one of the 'new' universities and opened other avenues of literary work. Like Samar, I decided to stay on in England. I was quite deracinated – I'd only been back to Karachi once for ten days in the late seventies, to see my sister (who'd landed a role in a TV serial – she'd wanted to act since her school days).

Aliza went back to Karachi after a year in Cambridge. We were lounging on the grass of Hampstead Heath on a Saturday with food and drinks around us when she announced that she wanted to help her people. Samar teased her about her relevance to today's Pakistan. Deconstruction in service of social reform?

Aliza was the firebrand of our group. Samar, the quietly cynical thinker with political theory at her fingertips, held that people like Aliza and herself would be redundant in Pakistan, especially at a time when things were the way they were for women and intellectuals.

'The best we can do,' she said, 'is to get scholarships or scrounge off our parents for a little longer and continue to study; then, if we can, we'll get jobs abroad. We can always travel back and forth on research grants. Over-educated women have no place there – we can get jobs as doctors, lawyers or architects if we accept that we'll be filthily underpaid.'

'That's your class-conditioning,' Aliza retorted. 'And what about all the fearless newswomen?'

'Class-conditioning tells us we can and should only go home to be successful in our careers as married women,' Samar said.

'Well.' Armaan raised an eyebrow. His scar was flashing. He'd been quiet until then. He'd quietly done an MA in area studies at SOAS, quietly abandoned the idea of doing a doctorate and was preparing to go home when his scholarship ran out. 'Aliza and I might get married one of these days.'

I hadn't thought much until then about Armaan's plans; I knew he didn't have much to go back to in Karachi. His brother had wanted him to study law; but because he loved Armaan he'd let him have his way, on condition he came back and did something for the ailing garments business that somehow still maintained his family. It seemed a waste, with his mind. But he was a promising writer. I consoled myself, knowing he'd be at home there in his own language: he'd switched to English for a while when he came here, but I told him his Urdu was far better, and if he had something to say to the world it was up to us to translate and publish it – we weren't even considering the readership at home in those days with our paranoid terrors of censorship. It also occurred to me for the first time quite how important Aliza was to Armaan – and how much more important they'd be to one another once they were home, how much closer they'd have to become.

Pragmatist that she was, Samar dismissed their ideals. But she agreed with me then that if they could fight the new repressive morality and cope with the stultifying older norms, they'd make a formidable working team.

'According to your own theories,' Samar said to Aliza that afternoon on Hampstead Heath, 'any revolution should rise among the proletariat or the peasantry. We're redundant. We should be the first to go. Even though we hold on to some beguiling old ways that keep a sense of culture and aesthetics alive in us, all that will have to give way to new forms, growing forms.'

'We came abroad only to educate ourselves to serve at home,' Aliza said. 'Many revolutionaries have been bourgeois anyway, many revolutions instigated by the bourgeoisie. It's up to us to go home and do some raising of consciousness ...'

'Among the oppressed, hear hear,' Samar sniggered. 'With Eco, Foucault, Derrida and Lacan as your fellow-liberators.'

'It's all part of a larger whole. You should be the first to know that! Linguistic philosophy has larger social ramifications. It reveals the place where the social and its structured codes come to dwell in the subject's psyche ...'

'All very well,' I interrupted: it was time to intervene. 'Let's cut the psychobabble and admit that what Pakistan needs today is technical expertise. If I were a technician I'd go back tomorrow!'

'Self-justification!' Armaan laughed. 'We've always had an intellectual tradition. It's just that your lot has to face the guilt that's eating you up, now you've left your marble palaces – my people never had very much to speak of, my brother used to study for his accountancy exams outside on the balcony by the light of a streetlamp at night to save money on electric bulbs.

What you can't do in your intolerable arrogance is to come home and become a part of some common everyday struggle. You set yourselves apart. I'm not asking you to be revolutionaries! Just come back and blend into life as it is. Try to make sense of it, fight if it's appropriate but at least fight for peace ...'

I fell silent. A picture of my sister formed in my mind. She didn't seem isolated, but I had the sense that with her husband and children, her voluntary work and her friends and her foray into amateur acting, she'd become a motif in someone else's tapestry. Hers was a life that reminded me of a rosebud embroidered on silk.

I shuddered.

3

But since Aliza and Armaan moved back to Karachi in 1982 I'd been to stay with my sister at least once a year. Sometimes I made three trips. I seriously studied contemporary Urdu poetry. I started to make excuses to myself for being there, not being there, everything ...

Aliza went to work for a women's fashion magazine and then into modelling. She said she'd rather exploit the system than be an underpaid social worker. You could see her, with her streaked hair, in outrageous outfits, in the social pages of every issue of the glossies for the first two years after she got home. Armaan, too – the husband from the wrong part of the city – was a hit in

Karachi. At first. He wrote for the papers, published two books of poems, read his verses in public, wrote plays.

In London, I had my teaching and some journalism on the side. Samar worked on the South Asia desk of an international human rights agency. We turned into outspoken public critics of the West. We discreetly criticised affairs at home but were careful not to say too much. Samar grew her shoulder-length hair down to her waist and refused to wear Western clothes; she bought herself a stunning wardrobe of regional homespun to wear to the conferences at which she was becoming a regular speaker on Third World political economies. She started to write her book about professional women in Pakistan.

'It's another of your late-capitalist luxuries,' Armaan said to me on one of my trips to Karachi. 'This guilt complex about their ex-minions. They feel that while we have a voice to shout with their principles of freedom of speech, democracy and self-expression have taken root in some of us. Hopefully, the token post-colonial will speak out against universal corruption without digging up the worst of their imperial secrets or saying too much.'

'If Samar's discreet it's because she loves Pakistan and even more than her country she loves her friends there.' I made a sweeping gesture in his direction and Aliza's. 'She wants to keep coming back.'

This was one of the first overtly political discussions we'd had since Armaan and Aliza went back to live in Pakistan. Armaan had been speaking with a measure of satire, of self-parody. I know he envied us our privacy in England, our solitude; he'd have liked that freedom to write, think, imagine without the constant stimuli of political events. He was a sociable solitary who had abdicated his right to dream – at least in the present – because he wanted to serve something he placed higher than himself.

I was in Karachi for the performance of his second play.

I'd read Armaan's script based on the Bokassa story. It worked well in the Brechtian mode, his monstrous story of a baby-guzzling despot, a diamond-distributing power-broker propped up by an ex-colonial regime. Armaan's treatment carried analogies far enough to hit where it really hurt: the modern masters of our destinies in every hemisphere were depicted as puppeteers constantly intruding into each other's shows. And his original idea was to present it all as shadow theatre, with live puppets.

Samar said: 'It'll only ever reach your intellectual cronies.'

Armaan took action, fast. He turned to the language that came naturally to him, realising as he wrote that his mental reflexes and syntactical processes had been conditioned by his academic training in English. So in Urdu he rewrote the play entirely, making it a collaborative affair, working with a multilingual group made up largely of amateurs. He took the play to slums and distant suburbs, making it street circus.

Even those intellectuals who weren't openly on the Left crept out of their airconditioned enclaves to have a look. Aliza – The Alleycat, of jeans and TV colacommercials and fashion-spread fame, with her multicoloured hair and hourglass figure, the highest paid model in the city who earned 10,000 bucks for a morning's work on a photo shoot and was also a Yale-and-Cambridge brain, was in it. The main attraction, some said.

The Urdu version was cruder than the English. Almost farcical. But it hurt. The analogies rung true. The lumpen elements, as our smart-arses called them, picked up every inference.

The smart crowd would arrive and take their seats, sit down in front of the white screen, look at the play of shadows projected. Then someone from the audience would turn around and cry out: 'You idiots, are you content only to gaze at shadows? Come and look at the other side, that's where it all happens!' Even I couldn't say whether it was a plant, someone from the company, or not. I saw the play twice: both times a few and then a crowd of people rushed over to the other side of the screen, where you could see the performers, wrapped in bright rags, wearing giant gaudy Kathakali masks.

The riots that took place around several factories may not have been directly connected with the play. The fact that the man who played Bokassa was a famous comedian and puppeteer and repeated some of the show's gags on the box hardly explained the reaction. Nor might Aliza's seemingly innocent slip of the tongue one night – she substituted the name Yazid for Bokassa – have been the cause. Unmasked and draped in a black veil, denouncing a murderous tyrant in the stirring language of Muharram elegy, she couldn't help recalling the women of Karbala. But then a famous right-wing comedian quipped in a variety show that he'd seen a group of factory workers beating up a bitch with a baton and calling her the General's whore mother, and he wondered who they really meant? The links between the street riots and the jokes about military regimes were finally apparent. A group of vigilantes broke up the platform and chased the performers offstage – many were badly beaten, and Aliza had a broken leg – but the players had done their work. The police came in and took everyone away in a van. But no one could blame the authorities for the end of the show: since the script had mysteriously disappeared the authorities couldn't do a thing and the performers were let off after one night in custody with a mere warning. But Aliza's father, who had paid a great sum to somebody to bail his daughter and son-in-law out, issued his daughter a warning that was far sterner.

By the time he sent us the bird manuscripts Armaan had begun to feel lost. We'd often asked him why he didn't get away, at least for a while. There was a writer's fellowship in Iowa. He'd actually grown to love Karachi, he said. And he loved travelling in the desert of Sind. That, to us, seemed something new, a revelation – when we were in Karachi we concentrated on food and friends, occasionally made trips to Lahore or Islamabad, or went to the seaside or holidayed in the mountains; we moaned about 'the backwardness of the interior' and 'the killing heat'.

When I thought of Armaan's love for Pakistan, I realised that the landscapes of the poems I'd started to write were unconscious and perhaps romanticised reflections of the topography of the Karachi I'd known as a child, which had now given way to new residential areas and high-rise blocks. Mango, papaya and guava trees, lines of camels, contrasts between the white of sand and the green of a palm leaf on a tree laden with dates, the green of the sea, the green of the sky at a certain hour ... and then there was that long-drawn cry to Allah that comes from the local songs, mixing ecstasy with awful longing, which never failed to rip out something raw from the hollow of my ribcage. Sometimes I think I'd never have learned to look at it all, to draw from that well of sounds and colours deep within me, if it hadn't been for the time I spent over Armaan's words when I worked on his *Hibiscus Days*, cutting and pruning and reshaping to give them form in the English I used so much more deftly than my own tongue. (It's been said I take undue liberties with Armaan's work. Appropriate it, to express my own thoughts. But in a way I think it's our book, *Hibiscus Days*; mine and his. I dedicated it to us all.) He certainly brought me back to the language I'd held at a distance, nearly forgotten, neglected for so long. But Armaan was obsessed with the music and the poetry of the life around him, the element of showmanship so evident in the minor lyricist, the singing camel driver, the gatekeeper who changed his occupation for a storyteller's bright coat of metaphors when the sun set on his day's work.

Wake up, wake up and smell the coffee, Samar would say to him, in a nasal mock-Brooklyn whine. Marxist friends of ours said

Armaan was returning to an aesthetic of blood and soil, that he was a nativist who in his writing – even in the cultural journalism he did for an income – was perpetuating an Arabian Nights scenario. The vignettes he was producing of his raggle-taggle friends in various walks of life were variations of the progressive realism that he'd briefly espoused as a boy when he was reading Urdu moderns, before he'd been exposed to articulators of the fantastic like Marquez or Borges or Rushdie, or theorists of literature as play, the comic as subversive. I argued with these detractors. 'He's given up on abstraction,' I said: 'he's portraying life as lived by people he feels close to, he's singing to us in the voices of those we never bother to listen to. He does what he, like every other poet, wants to do. He's making. Naming. Praising.'

But with all my loyalty and ardour I couldn't go very far in my defence of him. His radical admirers of past years called his political silence an espousal of bourgeois values, a compromise with the conservatives, a class-conditioned and individualistic response.

Talking about him to Samar I remember how we'd jeered at him, when he suggested some exotic expedition we'd never have dreamed of making, remembered the undercurrent he'd become a part of, the dives with their singing whores, street musicians, wayside stalls where a tobacconist might chant, all night, without forgetting one word, one sequence of Shah Abdul Latif's *Risalo* which he knew by memory. He'd stepped into that living river which, if you let it, just carries you on its tide.

A life that was vanishing. Fading from hibiscus red to a faint bloodstain on a well-washed bandage.

Hibiscus days he showed us, wrote for us, left for us to hold in our eyes. Hibiscus days and nights.

Armaan. We realised, Samar and I, that like the poets he loved, our own local poets who'd replaced the Baudelaires and Rimbauds and Rilkes he'd devoured during his English sojourn, he'd wrapped himself up in what was surrounding him as if it were a quilt to keep him warm in the desert night.

Singing and silence. The right to live in peace in a troubled land.

4

Back to the summer of '86. Now Armaan's new poems showed the stirrings of despair. I took it for a sign of the times: I didn't know it might be personal. He sent a note with the manuscript telling us he didn't want us to publish the poems and pieces in England or America, not yet. Samar wanted me to translate them for *Index on Censorship,* but, Armaan had written, that was 'fodder for the bleeding heart white liberals' who'd write him into a corner: Westernised intellectual silenced by a corrupt Third-World regime, implying that his rightful place was in Western exile and not on home ground. Samar and I were proving the post-colonial point by working in the West at explaining ourselves to the West.

'What', I could hear Armaan ask, 'will I do in England, away from all that means anything that to me? It's been like that since I first left home to study in England. I was different from all of you. Being away from here only made me determined to come back and do what I could. But I'd had to come away to relearn my dialect, my idiom; pitch it against the world's ideolect.'

'We all think we can speak to the teeming millions,' was the response of our sceptical democrat Samar. 'But talking to the 2 per cent hardly makes a difference if the swarm goes hungry – head and heart empty even if your belly's full. Bread and the strength to survive, that's what people need, especially women. You're not up to much as a social theorist, Armaan my darling. Your idealism is of the schoolroom variety.'

But when we'd seen him that winter before he sent us the manuscript he'd been talking again about his search for a voice in which to present the frayed fabric of a synthetic society. How public rottenness and private fears had become one in people's minds, making the interior life an inferno because you couldn't have an interior life with things the way they were.

In one of his fables, a man reflects:

> It's all a sham. You can't be alone without a hidden
> enemy. You don't need media images, you carry
> little portable screens in your brain, that you show
> you the chaos of madness and dread, madness that's

silent, the sort of dread that's worse than the hostility that the regime of a Hitler or a Stalin inspires. Much worse. Exchange your soul for guaranteed safety. A splinter of ice remains in your eye and you reckon that frozen bit of soul's enough to give you away to the secret police. Then feelings harden into fear, ice turns to steel. You're scared of yourself. But no one's really watching. It's all in your head.

I read it out to Samar on the terrace of our Primrose Hill flat. She tipped some more red wine – she never did realise how much I hated it, especially in summer – into her glass and mine. She sat with her feet up and crossed on her chair. Her hair was knotted up at the nape of her neck because of the sudden London heat. Her voice rose a decibel as it did when she was excited. Her thin fingers clutched at an absent breeze. She'd had a little more wine than she ought on an empty stomach. Talk of Pakistan – and Armaan – did that to her.

(And late one clear bright mid-March night by the sea, lying on the bone-white sand slashed with silver and littered with starfish, his head resting in the taut brown hollow between her belly and her breasts, Armaan told Samar about the bird poems. Standing in the balcony of the old colonial flat he lived in with Aliza overlooking the sea, he'd seen a bird, shot down by a child's sling; it flew past and smashed on the stones of the balcony below. Later, he said, a small child came onto the balcony and dipped his finger in the fresh death. The phrase, like so many of his phrases, caught her attention, but this was new ... pictures of blood, broken feathers, red lust, calculated to disturb as much of his conversation was. But there was something morbid here: he was talking about how perfectly the bird died, how its heart must have stopped in midflight. Samar told him he must have dreamed it all.)

5

How could we know that summer day in '86 that Armaan was dead? Aliza, though they'd been living apart for months, was in tears as she broke the news to us on the bad international line two days later. It was an accident, she said. Neither suicide nor an assassination (as some commentators implied). He was driving up a mountain path to Nathiagalli. A lorry drove his car off the road.

Some said he'd been drinking whiskey till late at a friend's house with a group of writers and poets.

In a covering note to the manuscript that arrived he said that after a writing block he'd written seventeen new poems in as many days. Those were the exquisite prose pieces I later shaped into the bilingual volume *Hibiscus Days*, love poems to a single woman and to the maternal body and the children of an entire country, poems that bring something vital, sour-sweet with the flavour of street talk, to our literature. It's a cult book. Strange that he wrote *Hibiscus Days* while he was breaking up with Aliza and producing those depressing verses about dying birds. Strange that Samar left me for a job in Canada while I was translating and shaping *Hibiscus Days* into a book. ('Stay with me,' he says, the night before Samar leaves Karachi: 'I need you, don't go back to London yet.' Typically, he isn't thinking about Aliza. He isn't thinking about me. Samar didn't talk to me about their days and nights together. I read his version in *Hibiscus Days.*)

Samar still works in Vancouver. (She didn't come back, though I said I was prepared to forgive, if not forget.) Aliza, who never again left Karachi for more than nine months, runs an NGO, a feminist publishing company – she publishes art books, tracts and the occasional novel, rarely poetry. In spite of their rivalry, she brought out Samar's second book. She never remarried. We've become close friends. We don't talk about Samar and Armaan.

And me – I didn't write the poems I wanted to. There are so many stories – about us all, and our hibiscus days – we have yet to tell. I spend most winters in Karachi. I'm done with what I have to say about the man who took away my dreams and my lover; he's dead, she's made another life. But I'm still translating and talking about the poet Armaan. Making a mission of keeping his words alive. And sometimes when I wake up in the morning I look in the mirror and I see, instead of my reflection, his face.

The Book of Maryam

It was the shortest day of the year. Poets, writers and thinkers were to gather to speak about the state of the world at a symposium about the role of the writer in troubled times. It was only a few nights before Christmas and they'd found it hard to book a room at the university as the holidays had already begun. And to make things more difficult the day they'd chosen was a Friday.

Murad had found out from a mail she'd sent him only a few days before that his friend Tahira, the celebrated and controversial poet from Karachi, would be stopping over on her way back from New York. He thought she'd be a perfect late addition to their gathering. He elected himself as reception committee and went off to Heathrow to pick her up on Thursday evening. But though he waited several hours she didn't appear. When he got home there was no message from her.

They made an announcement at the start of the symposium the next morning that Tahira would be reading at the end of the day. Before midday she called on Ayla's mobile to tell them she'd arrived. Should she take the tube from Heathrow? They told her to get a taxi and they'd pay at their end. She arrived forty minutes later, harrassed and hungry, and the taxi driver wanted fifty pounds. Ayla and Murad had been waiting for her on the stairs. Luckily, they had just about that much between them in their wallets.

They took Tahira to lunch at the nearby Italian sandwich bar which was the only place open, and watched her eat a heaped plate of pasta with pesto and chicken. It was 2.30 and the symposium was in progress. They'd have to miss a couple of presentations.

'They stopped me on my way out of New York,' Tahira told them. 'Though my entry papers should have been in order and I'd had no trouble getting in even with my Pakistani passport, they said they had no record of my arrival three weeks before – and I didn't have my letter of invitation any more, I'd handed it over to immigration. I'm not even going to tell you what they put me through for three hours, it's too tiring. Anyway, it turned out that I'd come in at the other airport and that was part of the problem. So I missed my flight and had to pay a cancellation fee ...'

The overcrowded classroom was painted white and lit with bluish neon. The only windows were very, very high and all you could see through them were squares of black. It was 4 by the time Tahira took her place. Her voice was slightly hoarse, and strong. She read an old poem, then a new one. Silence settled, punctuated only by applause, both surprisingly resonant in the rectangular, nakedly lit room.

Tahira read two more pieces: difficult to say if you could call them poems. One was about the wife of a policeman who was arrested for accepting a tiny bribe; to feed herself and their children, she'd taken part in a home-made porn video and been arrested too. The kids took to the street. The second was about two girls: one raped by Indian soldiers on a train while the staff looked on and cheered, the other, a twelve-year-old, raped by American soldiers in Taiwan. Tahira's readings had no obvious relevance to the war to come and Murad could sense some discomfort before a heckler with a black beard called out:

'This is reportage, journalism, agitprop, not art. What does it have to do with art or peace or poetry or the war to come?'

She ignored the heckler and went on with her reading. Her next piece was about a poet who was also a minor bureaucrat until he earned the disfavour of the current regime, how he was looked after first by the local prostitutes' union and then given a job in a leading businessman's office where he was led to a desk and told his task was merely to sit down and write. Though the protagonist was male, Murad recognised the latter anecdote as autobiographical.

Then a very fat man who looked like a fish that had been kept in a can for twenty years walked in. He wore a blue uniform with rows of buttons and was sweating heavily. He must have been some sort of janitor. He was shouting at them all: probably reminding everyone that their time in the building was over, which was fair enough, but the only word people could hear was fuck, fuck, fuck, and then the audience's intervention, about art and freedom and racism and police states. Tahira went on reading during the interruptions; she abruptly stopped when the fat man walked right up to her, left the platform and came down to the audience to grab Murad's arm. He led her out of the room, apologising.

'Not your fault,' she said.

They had to walk through a long corridor, lined on one side with what seemed like miles of plate glass. Outside it was blind-dark though it was only about 5 o'clock. Inside, the blue lights were switching off one by one. But blue glares lit them up from the outside. No one said very much. Two of the postgraduate students and maybe four or five others from the English Department had hung on while the others dispersed. They were leading Tahira and her friends to a place where they could have a drink and maybe even a sandwich as Ayla and Murad hadn't eaten. The students did all the talking.

They got to a cavernous brightly lit refectory, a place of steel, chrome and perspex. Tables swam in the light like mushrooms.

They sat down. Even before they'd got their drinks an Indian man was asking Tahira why she'd targeted Indian soldiers in her poem when it was, after all, Pakistan that was ruled by a military dictator. Tahira didn't reply; she just looked tired. So Ayla asked, probably to rescue the situation:

'Tell us. What are you working on now?'

'A translation into Urdu,' Tahira replied. 'Of my favourite poem. My version of it's called "The Book of Maryam".'

'We didn't really get to hear enough of you,' Ayla said. 'That bloody interruption. Could you read us a few passages?'

Tahira started, without hesitation, her voice very soft and pure, like a hymn or a requiem: '*How can I have a son,*' she said, '*when no man has touched me, nor am I sinful?*'

But Oliver the Redhead, who'd been poet-in-residence at the college that term, was also talking in a loud, flat voice.

'I had a dream last night,' he said. 'I dreamed I'd been invited to read in a country where everybody wore a veil and bowed a lot and talked about a Great Leader.'

'O yes,' said Violet, the Critical Theory person, in her Yorkshire voice. Tahira was still reading quietly:

> *The birth pangs led her to the trunk of a date-palm tree.*
> *'Would that I had died before this,' she said,*
> *'and become a thing forgotten, unremembered.'*

'They took me to a theatre much bigger than an ordinary theatre,'

Oliver went on. 'I was meant to read there but when I went to the stage, which was three times the size of an ordinary stage, it was full of dancers crowding around me. They were dressed in flowing robes of very bright colours, primary colours, purple and red and blue. They had veils on. Masks and half-veils and netted veils.'

'O yes,' said Vi.

Tahira had stopped her recitation. She had the same bewildered expression in her eyes as when the fat man had interrupted her reading. She had a fixed half-smile on her mouth.

'They flooded the stage', he said, 'and then they were waving banners. Banners with pictures on them and praise of the Great Leader. They had bells on, lots of bells, on the edges of their banners, their robes, on their wrists, on their ankles. They went jingle jingle jingle, they went ching ching ching, they went ...'

'O yes,' said Vi. Tahira was still silent, looking up, looking down, smiling slightly.

'And then?'

'Then I woke up.'

'But could you see the Leader's face? Saddam, I suppose?'

'O no,' Oliver said. 'The leader was veiled.'

Tahira and Ayla were nudging each other and laughing.

'Masters of the Universe,' Ayla said, before Tahira took up her recitation again.

> *Then a voice called to her from below:*
> *'Grieve not;*

your Lord has made a rivulet gush forth right below you.
Shake the trunk of the date-palm tree
and it will drop ripe dates for you.
Eat and drink, and be at peace.'

Tahira paused. There was silence for a moment. Then all the lights went out.

The Angelic Disposition

1

I was watering flowerbeds in the garden when my husband came
through the gate and said:

'You'll have to be strong. Your friend ...'

He didn't need to tell me whom he was talking about.

2

I've often thought about this: there are people who are born to
sorrow and others who learn to grieve along the way. I'm one of
the latter kind. But you were born to happiness. How shallow
that sounds. Perhaps I should say: you were born to make others
happy.

3

I first met Rafi Durrani – when? I'd seen him, heard him read his stories, long before I first spoke to him. Once, at a picnic, he sang a melancholy Punjabi wedding song. I remember the way he entered a room: swaggering slightly, and then he'd bow to the left and the right as if he were saluting the invisible angels, his thin tanned hand, raised in a salute, grazing his forehead.

He'd published his first collection of stories, *Restless Birds*, in '33, I think. Siddiq Saheb gave it to me to read. Rafi wasn't quite twenty. His writing was romantic, verged occasionally on the sentimental, but with a fresh lyricism I hadn't ever come across in Urdu fiction. People spoke of foreign influence and bourgeois sensibility. Then he published his second book. He was telling the same stories of lost loves and the frivolities of childhood, but his light touch was lighter still; in place of the early tearful undertow, the new stories were fragrant with mischief, redolent of laughter. Children played jokes, students tricked teachers, girls masqueraded as boys, boys dressed up in *burqas* to trick their mates. One story, in particular, I loved. A young teacher, down on his luck, travels to a big city to earn his living and meets a childhood friend who gives him a job as tutor to his sister who's preparing for an exam. The young teacher falls in love with his student – or rather, responds to her virginal advances. Their love is discovered and the boy is thrown out by the girl's father. But then the girl's brother arranges for the young lovers to elope.

They move to a native state, where the young couple both find jobs teaching the rulers' children. One day, the brother knocks at their door: his father has banished him too. The story ends with the phrase: 'We'll look after you now.' We don't know whether the voice is the hero's or the heroine's.

I'd started to write by then, but signed my essays with the androgynous 'S. S. Farouqi'. I, too, wanted to write a story, about a cousin of mine and the girl he fell in love with, who chose to marry his much richer best friend. But I felt guilty about liking Rafi's story, and about wanting to write a romantic tale myself, though mine was as close to the truth as Rafi's probably was.

Rafi was of medium height and medium colouring, and he seemed surprisingly weightless. In his world, darkness seemed not to exist. And yet I could recognise compassion in him, too: his wasn't the wit of callousness or disdain. He wasn't a Marxist; neither was I.

But to sing so blithely of love in a time before siege? Those were strange days. We – the scholarly, the teachers and doctors and lawyers – were trying to find a place in a world that we were increasingly aware was no longer our own; and we felt obliged to write about change, to write to change it all.

4

How I published my first short story, in 1936:

We were driving along the dirt roads from Fatehpur Sikri to Dholpur in April. The fields were bare of mustard and wheat, but along the way you could see high piles of chaff, of mustard seeds, and even higher piles of cow-dung cakes. It was the season of pumpkins and the fields were dotted with little yellow pumpkin flowers. Sugar cane saplings were still young but growing, growing. On the road, our car hit the mud-smeared rump of a hairy black piglet, which ran, bleeding and squealing, from our path. Our Hindu driver said: 'They'll bash it to death and eat it now. Those miserable untouchables. They keep them as pets. They let them out at night to eat all the rubbish they can find and then in the morning they take them to feed again at cesspools. When they're fat enough they set them on fire alive and eat chunks of their flesh while the wretches scream. If the pigs are wounded or die, they cook and eat them.'

A little way down the road, I saw a pond where egrets, their every move elegant, were washing their wings. Nearby, in a puddle or a ditch, a dun sow wallowed with her piglets around her. I'd never thought much about pigs before: when I was a girl, we weren't even allowed to mention them, they belonged with the other unmentionables like snakes and lizards and dogs. But I reached Dholpur that night and wrote. About a sow and her brood, the kidnapping of one of her piglets for food, the dispersal of the rest, the sow's lonely struggle to survive. I showed it to Siddiq Saheb, as I always did in those days. He didn't say much, just: 'Can't you make the sow into a bitch? Or a donkey? You know how we feel about pigs.'

It seemed pointless to explain to my pragmatic husband that that was the point, but then he said: 'It's a good story.'

'Story? It's an essay ...'

'It's a story. In your second draft you have to get rid of that arch and knowing tone.'

I went back to my draft. I wasn't deft enough a writer then to tell the story in a sow's voice. (Much later, though, I would write tales for children in the voices of a cat, a squirrel and a monkey.) But I came as close as possible to the sow's point of view, abandoning the bird's eye perspective of my first draft. The first editor went one step further than Siddiq Saheb: he wanted me to turn my Suwwariya into a pack-mule. The female condition was too raw a subject for a male: he thought S. Sultan Farouqi was a man, my sow a mask for a prostitute. Hindu readers, he remarked, would think I was writing about the lowest castes. My Suwwariya was abused by pigs and men alike. I decided then to use my own name: after that I would always sign my fictions Saadia Sultan. An Urdu women's magazine, the best known in Delhi, whose editor was a family friend and had published some of my essays, rejected it outright.

'It'll be banned', he said, 'for obscenity. Particularly if the writer is known to be a woman. Why not keep to your initials and send it to one of the progressive journals?'

The third editor I sent it to accepted it. He sent it back to me with some minor amendments and a series of delicate line drawings of fields, piglets and farmers. The pictures gave my story an innocent touch, underlined the elements I'd deliberately used and subverted, of a children's fable. I thought that effective. But the publisher ran the story without the drawings: too many pigs for Muslim sensibilities, he finally decided. The story got some attention. It wasn't banned, though some people did think it obscene, particularly from the pen of a woman. I wanted to know who'd done the drawings the publisher had rejected. Someone told me it was Rafi. The popular young writer – whose debonair manner boys envied or emulated, whose photograph on the back jacket of his book set college girls swooning as a movie star's would, whose voice on the radio programme for which he occasionally read his stories and reviewed current fiction kept housewives awake all night – was also adept with pen and ink and sketchpad.

I wrote more stories. It seemed, somehow, the next step, to turn my concerns into sharp little fictions. I wrote of characters and situations I knew. A tourist guide at the Taj who refuses a large tip. A shoeshine boy. A doctor accused of malpractice. A widow whose in-laws abuse and disinherit her after kidnapping her son. A girl forbidden to marry because her suitor is the grandson of a launderess. The only difference between my essays and my tales was of tone: if in the former I'd used irony and sarcasm to talk about social ills, in the latter I devised labyrinthine plots and coincidences to illustrate those ills and make them cohere as stories. My plotting must have owed something to the three-day story cycles I'd grown up listening to.

There was another story I added, as an afterthought, because my publisher told me my collection was too short and I also wanted another tale about an animal. I wrote down, as I remembered it, a story my mother used to tell: a man has a pet peacock in his garden. He ties it up in a bag and feeds it through a hole. Every now and then the master asks, 'Are you comfortable?' And the peacock replies, 'I am.' Then the rains come and with them a flock of peacocks. When the peacock in the bag hears the rain and the cries of his companions he, too, begins to cry, to want to feel the raindrops on his feathers and spread his wings, to fly to the top of a tree. He begs his master to let him go. I framed the tale with the exchanges of a child who wants a peacock as a pet with her mother who tells her the tale to dissuade her. I called it 'Thirst'.

Rafi reviewed my book on his radio programme. He was disdainful about most of the stories. The sound of coins dropping into the palms of the poor jangled too hard in his ears, he said, and the garments of my hapless heroines smelt of camphor. Then there was the too-comfortable moisture of womanly tearstains on my sleeve, and the pointing finger of my well-bred distance from my material. In my sketches – he called them that – I wasn't yet a storyteller: the reformer's zeal was too present in my work. But the fables he liked: the sow and her destiny, the peacock's longing.

'The lady should be writing for children,' he said. There was a dearth in Urdu of serious stories for children. (Ah yes, there was another story he liked, the prose poem I wrote in my own voice, about the pain of giving birth, to a child born dead.)

I wanted to meet him. I sent him the draft of a long story I stayed awake to write one night till the sun came up, of a princess who falls in love with a horse. When the horse elopes with her maid she follows them to the Land of Darkness to take her revenge. Rafi sent back the hundred pages with a few pencilled amendments and seven beautiful sketches. The book came out the next year. It was read with alacrity by children and adults alike. The rumour went around that I'd allowed Rafi to rewrite the story. But by then he was my best friend.

5

In any exchange of letters there's a writer and a reader: this is invariable. It's hard to explain. I have something to say, to impart, to confess. You listen. And sometimes you, too, start singing, your triumphs and your failures and your little tribulations. But you could be saying all this to anyone. You're writing to make me write, that's all. Between my letters, waiting for yours to arrive so I can write again, I don't sleep, I walk around the silent house in darkness, I write and erase, erase and write. When I write, it's only to you. I live my day for you, my sleepless nights for my letters. I walk barefoot on the wet grass at dawn and see the gaudy green of parakeet wings weave patterns among the tender green of leaves.

A dove in a niche looks like a painted miniature by Mansour. A passer-by kicks a puppy in a lane: it runs screaming to its mother's teat and for the first time ever I want to touch, to caress a dog. I string my words, one by one, on a thread, string fresh jasmine buds and tuberoses on it too, and then I count your words of response, one by one, like the amber beads of my rosary, my friend, my friend, my friend, thirty-three and then thirty-three and thirty-three again.

6

He wrote to me about his childhood when I told him which my favourites were among his stories, how well he wrote about children at play. His stories were a map of India undivided: he wandered around, from his native place in some unknown district near Peshawar to Delhi and back, from North to South and North again, Madras to Kashmir, Karachi to Dehra Dun, sometimes travelling for days to reach wherever his parents were posted from the boarding school in Lahore at which he spent the academic year. I, some years older, spent my early years staying in one place, a little estate – on the border of UP and MP. I was happy too. The youngest child but one, I studied at home: my father taught me Persian and some Arabic, from my mother I learnt Urdu, from an old instructress the Quran. Maths I acquired from my brother. I had no skills with the needle. My father taught at Gwalior, the biggest town nearby and only came home at weekends. In the holiday season we travelled around our region to visit our relatives, saw its lakes and rivers, dry land and flat land and sandy stretches and rocks and grassy hills, and always, in their huts, the poor with their cataracted eyes and their sores.

I married Siddiq Saheb when I was seventeen because they said he'd let me study. I was bony, dark and tall and not very pretty; I loved books more than the accepted womanly pursuits. Dr Siddiq Ahmed Khan belonged to a scholarly family from Bhopal, but had moved to Aligarh as a student, and then to Delhi to work in the new university; a steady, silent man, eighteen years older than me and a childless widower, he wasn't given much to speculation or reverie. In a way, he became another of my teachers. I'd started to write before we married but in our early years together, he'd suggest a subject for an essay, correct the odd ungainly phrase, and always tell me: 'Your writing is your own. Guard it.'

He'd show my work to his friends and, when the time came, send it out to publishers. We had no children except that one little girl who was born dead. Reading became my harbour. Siddiq was a professor of History and Arabic. I taught, too: children from all over our little campus came to me to learn Arabic, Persian, Urdu. I tried to teach the children of the poor along with my students but too often they'd escape me. In the afternoons, when Siddiq Saheb gave his lectures to forty or fifty students, I wrote; once a week I tried to learn to play the sitar, but since I had no great talent as a musician, I took painting lessons instead and was soon producing passable imitations of Abdurrahman Chughtai. In the evenings, I read. Philosophy, history, logic. I had little time in those years for stories. At twenty-two I wrote the book for which scholars of today remember me: a commentary on the writings of the eighteenth-century philosopher Shah Waliullah and his doctrine of man's twin nature, angel and beast; his constant search for an accord between the two. My book was an amplification of the dissertation for which, studying privately, I was awarded my degree. Critics said, of course, that my husband had written it: he hadn't corrected a word, though at times he'd told me where to fill in gaps. He would always be my finest editor, never a co-writer. (I didn't write another critical work until much later, my work on Iqbal and his images of the Fallen Angel which won me a prize, but by then I was a professor and rarely wrote fiction, except for children; I was in another city, India was a reborn nation, and all the ones I loved best were gone.)

It was after the book about Shah Waliullah was published that I turned to writing essays – comic, acerbic, satirical. I used what some might call my woman's eye, though until much later I withheld my first name, keeping only its androgynous first letter, so that I could publish in women's journals as well as men's.

Rafi's entrance into my life made me restless. A bold wind would fill my sails and I'd my word-boats would cross white waters and black. What didn't go into stories went into letters, but more often the letters went into stories. Rafi and I always wrote in ways that remained unalike but I feel that if he inspired me I, too, encouraged him. Ridding ourselves of our mannerisms, we found our voices, in counterpoint. As the stormy clouds of social evil which had overcast the skies of my stories dispersed to show the occasional fragment of blue, some light fell on a long and unknown road and I came closer and closer to ground truths, dust truths, earth truths. Rafi, in contrast, wrote air, wrote light. But how can we live without those?

7

Rashida Zafar. Asrarulhaq Majaz. Our contemporaries, the ones who died young. The boldest and the bravest of us. They were both, unlike you and me, on the far Left. I remember Rashida best, who was four years older than I was: I'd meet her at the occasional gathering of the Progressive Writers Association, which Siddiq Saheb and I attended. (Siddiq Saheb and I, fellow-travellers, never could drag Rafi to them. The Lefties don't think I'm a real writer, he'd say; too bourgeois, I am, and I don't drone on about despair.)

Rashida told me once that she'd admired my story about the sow. The rest of what I wrote was for housewives, the equivalent of making and breaking old gold jewellery and resetting lustreless stones. She was an activist, not an intellectual: she didn't have time for thinkers, with the exception of Marx and Freud. She was a doctor and a Communist and didn't believe in God. I don't think she'd have had time for my literary essays either. Her stories were of the sort Rafi hated, rocky and muddy. But for all their focus on women's bodily secretions he would never have found in them the stains of genteel tears.

Rashida died young, of cancer. It was anger, not grief, that made her write. Majaz, the firebrand anarchist poet, wrote out of fury too, about our cities and their desolate streets, our yellow dead moon like a priest's turban or the blush of youth on a widow's cheek. He died before dawn, a tramp drunk on a dustheap, on one of those mean streets which he'd written about in that long poem that became the anthem of our generation. He was about thirty. His fury was always intertwined with sorrow. He was one of those born to sorrow. As you were born to happiness.

Who causes us more pain? Those who, like Majaz, leave us grieving because they turn their youth into gunpowder? Or those who drive themselves in service of some greater good and are taken away too young by disease? Or those, like you, who leave a trail of happiness behind them like the scent of jasmine blossoms, and then disappear, one day, petals scattered on the wind? I'm using the clichés of the traditional poetry I could never write. (You, though you mocked it so adroitly, could spin reams of it impromptu in the rhythm and metre of the classics; you'd parrot the bombastic couplets of the reformists like Hali, parody the fragmented non-verse of a modernist like Majaz. You loved Mir and Dard and Zauq and Iqbal as much as you loved anything that had ever been written or recited. I still have the annotated edition of Ghalib's complete poems you left at my door before you went away.)

8

Rafi married. His wife had twin sons. He wrote another book, perhaps his best. I gave him its title, which seemed to fit: *The Angelic Disposition*. But in Rafi's world there were no beasts. Or even the animals and birds had angelic natures.

Rafi went abroad. War broke out in Europe, first the phoney war and then the real: we felt it coming close in '41. Rafi was fighting, flying. His letters stopped coming. What made him join Britain's Airforce? He'd never been openly anti-British like Siddiq Saheb, nor a homespun nationalist like I was, but we always felt he sided with us against the imperialists. What dream of freedom and resistance took him up into the air on war's wings? The love of universal liberty, equality and fraternity? Or the promise of our freedom after we'd sacrificed our lives to someone else's war?

I felt Delhi's red stones weigh down on me now. People forget sometimes that it's a city of monuments, so many of its most exquisite structures tombs, in so many other places – forts, palaces, gardens – tactile shadows of uncounted defeats; reminders, too, of the failed uprising that led to the decimation of a people. I couldn't breathe there. Even the grandiose architecture of the buildings the British had erected echoed, clumsily, the memorials of the past.

I'd always grown up near water; the Jamuna, known to us quite simply as The River, flowed beneath my father's house, just a hundred steps from our back gate, and I'd played there until I was old enough to veil myself, which I did for a very few years before my marriage, but even then, in the evening, with the women of my family, all of us draped in large shawls, I'd walk along its banks. When the tide ran low, local people would use the fertile soil to plant watermelons and cucumbers. The very same river flowed in Delhi, too, but it had started to run dry; in summer, especially when it didn't rain, it was reduced to a trickle, barely enough for washermen to rinse their piles of soiled clothes in its yellow-brown water. How could we live, I'd ask myself, in such a big city, without a limpid river, without a great body of water?

My restlessness turned into listlessness. I couldn't read or write. I'd always tried to say my prayers five times a day whenever the day's tasks allowed; if I missed a prayer or two I'd say several of them at one time. I remember how, more than once, the words 'Compassionate and Merciful' with which we begin our prayers had brought tears to my eyes, tears that hurt and left me shaking though they were, in a way, tears of joy, and I had to distance myself from that passion but afterwards I'd feel as if I'd been in a cool, cool torrent of rain, or bathed in a waterfall after a very hot day, then dried my wet skin on a piece of the bluest sky. But now if I knelt down to pray I'd see terrifying pictures, they'd burn my closed lids, and the Arabic words would run from my mind.

Once Siddiq Saheb came home from work and found me

crying for no reason. He asked me why and I said I was like that peacock in my mother's story, longing for the rain and the sky, but I couldn't hear the music of the rain, I didn't know why the cries of my peacock mates had fallen into silence, and I didn't know where to go and spend my longing.

He took me away from that moribund Delhi winter. I'd accepted visits to shrines in my early years as something traditional women did, and in Delhi I'd only ever visited Nizamuddin's tomb not far from where we lived once, but now I felt the Chishti saints were calling me. He took me, my gentle husband, to Fatehpur and to Ajmer. At Sheikh Salim's shrine two singers were celebrating the light within us and around us, their enraptured notes seeming to soar towards the midday sun. I tied a string to the latticed wall of his tomb and said, 'O God, bless the saint and bless the ones I love. And I am a tangled skein in your hands, untangle me.'

We went to Ajmer. I threw fistfuls of rose petals on Sheikh Moinuddin's tomb. At the grave of his daughter, I felt a hand on my shoulder, a cool breeze on my forehead. When I turned, no one was there. I paid the water carriers to pour water from their waterskins into the pool. Then I saw Rafi standing there, in a green shirt, clothes of a local cut. I ran towards him: I called out. He turned, smiled, and didn't answer.

'Who were you calling out to?' Siddiq Saheb asked. 'There's no one we know here.'

9

In a story I'd go back and find you'd come home. I expected you to knock at our door. But you didn't, not then: you came home eleven months later, on leave. You came to visit in your Airforce uniform. So difficult to speak when you're used to writing, to stringing words on fragile chains and watching while they swing, swing. You looked into your white china teacup. My husband went in and out of the room. You stayed silent. You jabbered. You recited poems. You'd published some detective stories, set in the high places of Indian cities, in a journal; you wanted to write some more, and make a book of them. You'd been reading Evelyn Waugh and P.G. Wodehouse in England. You left copies of their novels for me to read, forgetting, perhaps, what a chore it was for me to read English then, and how boring I found its fiction. I forgot to tell you that I was working on that novel I'd wanted to write for so long, and you were my intended reader.

I never asked what you'd been doing or even where you might have been that day in December when I thought I saw you in Ajmer.

You left. On active service. You went to war. You didn't write for months. In 1944 I got your last letter.

Nine to ten weeks after that my gentle husband came home and found me watering the flowerbeds in our little garden. He told me: 'Saadia, you've got to be brave. Your friend ... Rafi Durrani was shot down near the Burmese border three weeks ago.'

I didn't say a word; I tripped, and the watering can fell to the grass. I remember water spilling on green blades and some trampled mauve flowers. Siddiq Saheb took me to the sitting room, to the armchair where he usually sat. Sprinkled water on my forehead from a glass, made me a cup of strong salted tea with his own hands.

10

The second distinctive trait of man ... is his aesthetic sense. While a beast wants that which may quench its thirst and satisfy its needs, man often requires contentment and pleasure beyond his instinctive needs ... The second stage of social development is possessed by people living in civilised cities belonging to those virtuous realms that raise men of morals and wisdom. In such places human social organisation tremendously expands, giving rise to increasing requirements ... the third stage ... is reached when various transactions take place between human beings in this society, and elements of greed, jealousy, procrastination, and denial of each others' rights crop up, giving rise to differences and disputes. In such a state of affairs, there appear some individuals who are ruled by low passions and are disposed to commit murder and loot ...

So said the sage Shah Waliullah.

11

People write about the dead. His sister and his friend Razia wrote about Majaz. Rashida's husband, and so many others, those who knew her and those who didn't, wrote about her. They forgot you. And I never wrote about you. What would I have said? I kept a diary, hoping to celebrate our freedom from the British. Instead, I wrote about discovering how much I loved Siddiq Saheb after he fell under some fanatic's pickaxe on a Delhi street: the bastard didn't even know whom he was killing, just slaughtered a Muslim as an object of his hate. (Siddiq Saheb had gone to the slums with a group of others, Hindus and Muslims, to stop the rioting. He didn't let me go with him. He'd sent me into hiding, in another town. I came back to Delhi, despite the dangers, as soon as I heard the news. For three years at least I wished I'd been with him till the end.) Only ninety years after the last pogrom, another: this time, something like a civil war, and many said the departing foreign rulers had carved up the country so badly that it had to be that way. I'd always written carefully, almost cautiously, but now my words came like a haemorrhage, leaving me dizzy and drained, but then some other image of devastation would come back to me and I'd find the flow had gone; I'd have to prick myself, fingertips and breast, to extract drops of blood for ink in which to write. I wrote about seeing the camps of those who'd decided not to leave Delhi, the destitutes in the Old Fort, my attempts to work with old Gandhi whom, like any other leader, I couldn't really bring myself to trust. People told me how others had died in Punjab, Hindus and Sikhs, and I tried to see in their wan faces and battered bodies the mirrored sadness of my own departing people; but some of the refugees, too, were killers. In such times, whom does one condemn? Whom forgive?

Your dream, though you loved Delhi so much, was to go to live in Lahore, where you'd been to boarding school and then to college. Maybe you weren't meant to see the carnage in your country. Maybe the war and what you'd seen was all you could bear. The nature of angels you believed in, the nature of beasts you could never bring yourself to describe. (The devil, too, we're told in the first chapter of the Holy Book, was once an angel. He refused to bow down to Adam, God's perfect creation. God exiled him from the garden. He pledged to tempt all but the truest souls to perdition. God let him go his way, where he wanders, leading us into his temptations.)

What did you reckon with in your last hours, before you left us? Did you recognise the devil and the beasts?

Maybe angels should never grow old.

12

Like Ghalib in 1857 – though not with his grace – I'd wanted when I edited my journal into a book and sent it to my publishers to bear witness to my time. Still more, to write a testament of grief for my husband, to the lost ideals he represented. But no one wanted to publish my book. Sprinkling salt on open sores, they said in that euphoric post-national moment.

So many of those I cared for most, my brothers and sisters and friends, were leaving Delhi, Aligarh, Lucknow; some because they wanted to go, some because they had to. Some, the brave and the patriotic, stayed on. I had nowhere to leave for, no patriotism for any place.

Restless again, I went back to the shrines of the saints from which I had once returned so serene. But when I was there I asked my maker and his messenger and the saints: What have you done to us all, to my lost ones, to the dead? There was no gush of cleansing tears, my eyes were dry. I had come to believe only in the beastly disposition. My angels had gone their way.

I took a train to Lahore the year after my friend Rashida died, in '53, and from there a train to Karachi. I travelled nearly three days. I was forty-two years old and I'd lived in Delhi since I was seventeen. We'd just about managed on Siddiq Saheb's pittance of a salary and my earnings as a teacher and a journalist, but now, as a widow without a pension, I was destitute. My brother, who'd sent me the train fare, found me a job in a women's college there. I lived with his family in Bath Island, not far from the sea, which sometimes wafted the salt odour of fish through our open window. It took me time to get used to the camels and the date palms and the sandstorms and the sea.

I published my memoir in '61. They gave it the title *Partitions*;

I'd called it *The Nature of Beasts*. I did my doctorate at fifty, on the influence of Rumi and Shah Waliullah on Iqbal's metaphysics. I wrote about Iqbal's vision of Iblis, the fallen angel, the adversary who claimed to love God more than any of His creations; that, too, became a book. I've lived in Karachi since, neither foreigner nor native, but a citizen. (I'll be buried here, too, when the time comes.) About my involvement in social services and the local assembly to which I was elected and my internal exile during the Zias years, I'll stay silent. I'll abstain, too, from describing the pleasure of watching my brother's children grow, and how I realised, when they became adults, that they'd only notionally been my children, and the notion was mine alone.

In my sixties, when Pakistan was thirty-odd years old and once again divided, I painted and exhibited. When that peacock longing came back sometimes, I'd always painted, anonymous shadowy forms, hunchbacks with downcast faces and veiled figures in shadowy colours, but in their shadows, which people read as metaphors of national darkness, I sometimes glimpse an unintentional resemblance to something I've lost: a smile, the angle of a shoulder, the turn of a neck, a black lock falling on a forehead.

For a long time I missed that husband whose affection I'd soaked in through my pores and never consciously returned, accepting it as my natural reward. I missed him in that way you never know you'll miss someone who has always been with you till they're gone. Now, when I'm alone sometimes, I feel he's with me.

For a while I felt I should have gone to live in Lahore, the city in which, though he lived so long elsewhere, Rafi set some of his finest stories. But Karachi was a city where no ghosts waited for me. At the time I left I couldn't have faced another city that, like Delhi, still stank of death.

13

It was thirty years before I saw Delhi again. I'd finally completed the novel I'd abandoned because I felt there was no one left to read it after Rafi and Siddiq Saheb died. I'd stopped painting when my sight started dimming, and found the manuscript hidden between the pages of an old album, reading it with the interest with which one reads the work of a stranger and hears the remote echoes of a lost, familiar voice. I went back to work on it, changing little of what was there but adding several new chapters to it because I'd forgotten how it was meant to end. Somehow, I felt, it was a tribute to my lost ones, to whom I dedicated it. After a warm reception in Pakistan it had been published in India as well, in Urdu and in Hindi. People had almost forgotten I'd ever written fiction; the books on Iqbal, Walliullah, and Partition (all translated into English), a handful of stories and retold folktales for children – and my paintings, too – were what I was known for to two or three generations. But my two names, Dr Saadia S. Farooqi for my non-fiction and Saadia Sultan, with which I signed my paintings, made many people think I was two women. At one point a fine young woman wanted to publish an English translation she'd done of 'The Sow' in an anthology of women's writings, but in that odd climate of military censorship they asked me if I couldn't make my Suwwariya into an ewe or a she-ass and I, once again, refused.

My novel started with the line, 'I was watering flowerbeds in my garden when my husband came through the gate, put his hand on my shoulder and said ...' But it wasn't about Rafi. It was about a young man, mischievous, but sensitive, something like I imagined Rafi to have been as a child or a youth, who loves his cousin. He goes to the city to make a living for himself, as a writer and radio artist, and when he has his first success he receives a note from his childhood friend to say he's marrying the girl the hero loved and left behind. Later, he dies.

It's told from three points of view, the woman's, the man's, his friend's, and finally the woman's again. Strange, but the husband's voice is my favourite: he marries his best friend's beloved and spends his life regretting the pain he's caused. A story (if there is a story, rather than a sequence of events) so much like one of Rafi's. But mine is over three hundred pages long, laden with the sort of tableaux Rafi delighted in when he read my prose, of births and marriages and male pursuits and womanly things.

Just as they'd read my memoir of my husband and my widowhood as a document of Partition, they saw this anachronistic love story, this fantasy of youth, as a memorial of undivided India and its vanished gentry. I admit it's a world peopled with shadows. I couldn't summon them back, all the ones I'd loved, only their shadows.

I was seventy-two when I went back to visit Delhi. In a city now strange to me where my friends were geriatrics or phantoms and the places of my past were derelict, some young journalist asked: 'Why don't you write another volume of your memoirs? You had so many illustrious contemporaries, Rashida, Majaz, Ismat, Anis Begum, Faiz, Manto, Rafi ...'

I said, I remember them well, Rashida was the Communist and doctor, who spent her life in service to a greater good and whose ideals, in the end, were grander than any earthly love, though she refused to traffic with heaven; and Majaz was the anarchist firebrand, who, in the end, drove everyone away from his fire and was consumed by his own flames, as if he could only find redemption on the devil's path from the torture of the world around him.

But what could I say about Rafi? That he keeps company with angels?

Ours was a friendship that began and ended with letters. In between those, a fistful of meetings. How many times, after all did I meet him, talk to him alone, see him face to face? Seven times, nine, over about as many years? His letters to me I keep, and sometimes I've thought of collecting them into a little volume, but they amount to little more than a chronicle of daily events, with the odd quotation from something he was reading, or a word of encouragement to me about some idea for a story I'd mentioned. It's his spidery writing, peppered with English words in capitals, I study once in a while; and I contemplate the handful of pen-and-ink sketches of me he made on bits of scrap paper: sometimes while I was there and didn't realise he was sketching me, because he was so often doodling with a pen in his hand, and sometimes from his memory's eye (I know this now and think of it with pleasure). These things bring back more about him than any portrait.

And my letters to him? God knows where they went. His stories, and his comments on my writings, were how I knew him best. I wonder what he did with my letters, whether he kept one or two with him, carried them in a pocket or a wallet wherever he went. I wish I could have those letters of mine back to see the person I was then, the I that Rafi, in so short a while, made me imagine into being.

What remained of his presence I put into Saif, my novel's mild-mannered, slightly melancholy hero. Another of my failures. The tenderness and laughter and light that were Rafi I couldn't recapture. But I did give my hero one of Rafi's characteristics – I'd noticed it every time I saw him – on one of his long thin hands, the left, a malformed little finger.

Insomnia

When leaves turned yellow and red and began to fall my friend Murad felt autumn bite. He took his leather jacket off its summer hanger, put on cotton jumpers and socks every morning for a week, and prepared himself for a cooler season. He booked a ticket that would take him to the warmer clime of Delhi in winter, but he had nearly two months to wait before he could leave. Walking down London's grey streets in early October, he felt that something was about to happen: to him, to someone else, to the earth. But sometimes he thought, with a measure of guilt, that his own unease was big enough to keep away the problems of the world.

Friends from abroad came and went. Days of work were followed by evenings of celebration, and time sped. But when he came back late at night or even when he stayed home to work Murad couldn't sleep or read. He'd sit up till dawn in the darkened kitchen or speak on the phone to friends in countries where the sun hadn't yet set or had already risen. And when he did fall asleep his sleep was restless, his dreams crowded with strange journeys and occurrences. He'd shake himself into consciousness, switch on the lamp and fall back into a sluggish half-awake state with the reading light on. Or he'd go to sleep with fully formed stories in his head and on his lips, but when morning came and he tried to find the words to write them he could no longer remember what language they'd been in, if they'd been in any language at all.

One Saturday morning he dreamed that he was at a window, watching a group of survivors emerging from the debris of an earthquake, some of them carrying their dead on their backs. From somewhere he could hear the sound of an unfamiliar bell. He shook himself awake to find that he was lying on his back, in his shirt and suit trousers, his jacket beside him, on a strange bed. His socks were on and his shoes were off. In the dull light of the lamp beside him a TV screen showed men in white playing some rough ball game he didn't recognise. He had been woken by the harsh music of a mobile phone near him that wasn't his; he didn't have a phone near his bed, and would never have gone to bed with a mobile beside him.

'Oh you're awake,' his friend Saad said, walking into the room with wet hair and a towel round his shoulders. Shaking off his sleep, Murad remembered now how, after a reading they'd done at the South Bank followed by a slew of questions from the audience about abandoned mother tongues, nostalgia, the exilic and the exotic, they'd been out with some English friends, danced until late and then gone back for a drink to the hotel on Southampton Row where Saad and Ratna, the poet from Bangalore who'd read with them, were staying. Ratna had drunk rather too much white wine, and insisted on coming to Saad's hotel room to raid his mini-bar for a nightcap when the waiter in the hotel lobby refused to serve them more drinks. (At some drunken moment earlier in the evening, a pianist was playing dizzy cascades of jazz notes in a very minor key and Saad was fervently defending Michel Houellebecq to a sceptical Murad as the real voice of Europe when Ratna had looked up from a reverie, wagging a forefinger: 'Have you realised we're all middle-aged, single or divorced, and childless?')

'You must have fallen asleep when I took her up to her room,' Saad told him. 'You didn't even wake up when I pulled your shoes off.' Murad had a faint memory of taking off his glasses, rubbing his eyes and resting his head on a strange pillow. He had probably slept then. (He'd had only five hours of sleep the night before; a call from a sleepless friend in New York, who had left Karachi in 2001 and was still anxious about the change of city and career he had made in his late thirties, had wakened him well before sunrise.)

Saad, a Pakistani poet and human rights activist based for a while in Prague, was supposed to leave with Ratna to read that evening at a university in some distant northern town. He said Murad might as well join them for an early breakfast, but Murad excused himself. It was 7. On the way to the tube station, in the dull emptiness of Tavistock Square, he stopped to smoke in the abandoned park just across the road from where a bus had recently been blown up and remembered how, more than a decade before, he'd been sitting there talking to someone he'd recently met at a conference. Her name was Sri Kunti. Her small, perfectly crafted poems had beguiled him with their deceptive intimacy. She had brought boxes of rice, fried chicken and curried beef to the park, which they ate, kneeling on the Bloomsbury grass, with their fingers. She was leaving the next morning for Indonesia. The grass had made him sneeze. She'd told him she was allergic to most metals, particularly gold. Their meeting had inspired both of them to write. For seven months after that they'd exchanged letters, soaring into poetry or dipping into prose, before they were able to meet again, when she had him invited to present a paper on Iqbal's philosophical poetry at a conference in Leiden.

Why, he wondered, was he so often drawn to poets? Once – he was much younger – he'd heard them referred to as vagabonds, wasters and wanderers; in his experience, they did have a rather different approach to life, stability and structure. Sitting in the top deck of the bus, he succumbed to a remote regret for an ailing friendship with Ayla, a poet for whom he had once felt a poignant affection; their ambivalent relationship, after drifting for a while between the still pond of friendship and more stormy waters, had recently run aground. All new loves, Murad had told Ayla once, were re-enactments of old passions, revisitings of old pain. In her case, she wasn't able to engage in a new relationship because she hadn't managed to deal with the things left behind by a past one. He'd last seen her in June in Milan; there, at a performance of *Othello*, he'd said an imaginary goodbye to her, but after feeling there was nothing more he had to give her because there was little left she wanted from him, he was still aware of an empty place inside him where something else had once been.

'Didn't you examine your feelings for her?' Saad had asked him on the phone, in one of their late-night conversations. He thought he had, but he hadn't quite known what it would be like to live with yet another empty place. He sought refuge in friendship or solitude just as he had once sought solace in her company from those things, but he'd had a few too many of these evenings that ended too late after drinks in some club, hotel bar or friend's sitting room. (In a faraway town a month or two ago, he'd spent a night in the arms of someone he'd seen for years as a cordial stranger; their almost accidental love-making had remained, by tacit consent, incomplete. They'd parted with a promise to seek each other out more often. He'd thought this sudden intimacy might lead to something lasting, but all that came of it was a handful of messages and phonecalls, and two awkward meetings over drinks in crowded, impersonal places. Intimacy, perhaps, had precluded a possible friendship. It had occurred to him then how sometimes, even with eyes wide open, you could wilfully misread another person's needs, motives and messages.) Filling the spaces left empty by passion with friendship always made you aware of how the love of friends came in fragments: it could be confusing, and after initial intensity follow the usual sequence of delays, cancellations, eventual neglect.

He reached home. Oh, for one night of sleep. Eight hours, or even seven, uninterrupted by dreams, bells, voices ... At nearly 8, it was too late to go to bed. He made some coffee and checked his messages; he switched on the TV in the empty flat and, over flickering pictures of death and the stricken faces of victims, he heard a voice describing an earthquake in his native country. Surely he couldn't have had a premonition of the catastrophe? Then he realised that he'd probably seen an early report on the TV in Saad's room as he drifted into unconsciousness and thought he'd been dreaming; or that the images of the disaster had somehow imposed themselves on his dream.

Watching the world's tumult in miniature, in your sitting room, with the cold voice of a distant announcer in your ears, can trivialise tragedy, make it unreal, numb the spectator. He stretched out on the sofa to try to sleep but couldn't. And when he finally slept again he found himself in a half-darkened cell, being interrogated by two blond policemen who force-fed him a truth serum; to what crimes he was supposed to confess he didn't know. Then he was strapped to a very tall ladder; he was struggling to free one hand, the left, to reach into the pocket of his trousers in which he was sure he had a cigarette or two and a box of matches.

The phone woke him. 'O God, O God, O God,' a friend who'd recently lost a loved person was sobbing down the line: she hadn't wept at her bereavement, but she'd seen the news of the disaster and was crying now. And it occurred to him how, in dark places, the world's griefs and our own could melt into one another and become the same.

When he'd put down the phone after attempting to console her, his voicemail rang him back with another message: a doctor friend from Karachi was trying to reach him, with a list of places to which he could immediately send financial or practical help. He crouched by the phone, his head in his hands. Then he clenched his fists and drummed, with the sharpness of his knuckles, his forehead and his temples. When his head began to throb he flattened his fingers and kneaded the places he'd been drumming, and rubbed his itching, swollen eyes as if to demand from them the water they refused to yield.

He'd been invited out to lunch – it was a Saturday – but by 10 he knew he wouldn't make it. He phoned to cancel, pleading a painful knee and a pile of student papers to mark, both of which were true.

There'd been a message on his machine from Sri Kunti a day or two ago, from Lisbon. She'd accepted an invitation to read in Cambridge and Norwich and would be arriving in England soon. As usual, she wanted to meet him in a new and distant place. But she hadn't said when she was arriving, and he didn't know where to find her. Over the last eight years, he'd travelled to many places to meet this darkly enigmatic Javanese poet who many years ago had left behind her native aristocratic milieu for the world of ideas, books and academic seminars. Sri Kunti, the mother of twins like her namesake, was a nomad with a nesting instinct. One of her hidden talents was for architectural design, and in the last decade she had made nests in Bali, Amsterdam, Paris and other places, many of which he'd visited.

Their last meeting but one had been in the hills high above Yogyakarta, where, in the opulent surroundings of a tea plantation that had been transformed into a holiday resort, he had spent Christmas Eve with Kunti and her friends. On Christmas day they had driven to the sea, to a place called Parangtritis, where the ancient Queen of the Waters, Lara Kidul, was supposed to reign and did not allow people to dress in green, her special colour. Sitting on the patio, in the purple darkness of a late evening, with a huge platter of local fruit on a low table beside them, they'd been talking about happiness, and Murad had said: 'Why do we only know we've been happy after the moment has gone? Do regret for the past and fear for the future erode every possibility of recognising the moment?'

Kunti had smiled and responded in one of her cadenced reflective sentences: 'Sometimes you're listening to music, or looking at a landscape, or simply sitting in silence with someone and that feeling – you can call it happiness – overwhelms you. The saddest thing is to find out later that the other wasn't even aware of what you felt … didn't share your happiness at all.' She was silent for a moment. In the distance, Lara Kidul's dark sea raged and roared, buffeted by winter rain. 'Why don't you write a story about all that,' she asked in that deep, soft voice for which she was famous: 'regrets, fear, loneliness and joy – and set it right here, in Central Java, and in Bali, by our hills and by our sea? And call it, with just a little irony, "Happiness"?'

The next morning he'd said to her: 'I woke up last night with the vague idea that one of my ancestors, a Sufi preacher, was buried near here. I know one did travel to Central Java hundreds of years ago. I don't think it was a dream and I don't believe in summons or premonitions, so it must be some unconscious memory. I know it's silly, but could you ask … ?'

She wasn't surprised at all. And her queries proved the truth of his intuition. She arranged for Santo, the thoroughly modern but quietly religious young man who'd driven them there, to take him up to the saint's tomb, a local place of pilgrimage less than a mile away from the hotel. She sat in a café at the bottom of the hill with a pot of ginger tea as he walked up the several hundred steps that led to the small, simple white shrine where Santo said his prayers and he, who had never learnt Arabic or memorised more than a few verses of the Koran and only ever prayed without words or even a recognisable language, made a vow at the saint's tomb and asked for the return of light to his mother's eyes which had been dimming.

Exactly a year later, a tidal wave had hit the Indonesian coast, and in the aftermath of that devastation he hadn't seen Kunti again for months, their exchanges limited to telephone conversations when it was midnight where he was and a little after dawn for her. (On Christmas day in Partangtritis she'd given him, as a gift, a watch with twin faces: the hands of one were set at Jakarta time, so day and night he'd always know what hour it was there and what she might be doing.) Then, this summer, they'd met after a separation of eighteen months by the shores of Lake Como, bringing along unfinished manuscripts and untended stories to show each other. She was giving a paper at a conference that commemorated the centenary of the birth of the poet and philosopher Lidia Belluno, who had written, in this very hotel, her *Treatise on Friendship and Platonic Love*, a work of existentialist philosophy disguised as a series of letters, the book on which, along with a handful of poems collected after her death, her substantial cult reputation was based. Belluno and her friend and mentor Bruno Cavagna would sit side by side on the lake's shore and write. Cavagna was working on his masterpiece *Insomnia*, a tragicomic love story inspired by their friendship, which came out on the eve of World War II, was promptly banned, and only resurfaced in the fifties. Cavagna was married, Belluno wasn't. Later, reading the poems his muse had written as she sat beside him on a stone bench by the water, he'd realised the desire and hurt she'd been concealing from him. They became lovers. But only for a short while. She was too volatile for him. He, a Partisan, disappeared during World War II. But she'd already taken her own life by then, soon after he went back to his wife: friends and biographers of both said the transition from friendship to passion and then separation proved too much for her. Haunted by the story of Belluno and Cavagna, Murad started to work on his piece about happiness on the veranda of his hotel. He spent a lot of time looking at the fountain in the piazza and the play of light on the lake and gulls flying over silver water and ducks afloat. He didn't get very far beyond an allusive opening passage about the dead poets.

One evening Kunti and he had escaped their colleagues; they were eating cuttlefish in its own ink on the lake's other shore, and talking about Lidia Belluno's response to the war – which Kunti described as pacifist, since Belluno, while castigating the Fascists for invading Ethiopa, had really only thought of the cost to Italian mothers of their sons and to their sons. They'd missed the very last ferry and had had to hire a boat to take them across the lake. As they crossed the water, still talking about Belluno and Cavagna, with the sharp wind throwing foam in their faces, Kunti had asked: 'And your story, "Happiness"?'

Kunti often commented: 'My poems are quite prosy; they're actually stories. But you write poems in prose.' In fact, Murad had abandoned serious attempts at poetry twenty years ago, but he'd often envied his friends who were poets; even on tour or in transit, they seemed to disappear into hotel rooms and come back with poems written out of their overflow or their empty places, while his prose-writing friends locked themselves away for days, months and years on diets of cigarettes and tea, to write those masterpieces they dreamed would take them to pinnacles of acclaim, or they'd grieve over mountains of rejected manuscript. (A poem, of course, could be only three or four lines long but stories tended towards length, and though he was experimenting with lineation and layout to give himself more freedom, he had no interest in rhyme or metre: he thought that even if he did turn to verse, he'd write long, ragged poems.) Poetry or prose, it was all, in the end, a matter of working with pain, turning its blood and bones into something beautiful.

He hadn't known what to say to Kunti about 'Happiness', because he'd only gathered together scattered pictures that, on sleepless nights, he'd tint in the colours of happiness. (He's stealing a peach in an Italian orchard at the age of twenty, feeling protected by the gaze of a friend to whose passion he can't respond. He's driving up the winding roads of hills in Bali or Java with the lush green foliage, date and coconut palms, hibiscus and wild roses of the tropics filling his eyes and the music of wind chimes, church bells or the muezzin's call in his ears. He's sitting in a pavilion in the hills above Jogja with Kunti while the silver notes of the gamelan orchestra, intertwining with the unearthly shimmer of the singers' high-pitched voices, fill the hall with songs from her childhood – and one melody, 'Bengawan Solo', she's requested them to sing because he remembers it from his. He's looking from his hotel window in Cernobbio at the fountain in the square in which a duck swims and a gull and a white dove perch on successive tiers, forming a three-levelled sculpture. He's walking in the rain to buy cigarettes in spring on his thirty-first birthday when a pear blossom, like a snow flake, turning on the wind, drifts towards him and he cups his hand to catch it before it touches the pavement, wanting to give it someone but not knowing whom to gift it to.) You can spin stories out of your emptiness, but writing your images away can also leave you drained and empty. ('Where's the writing today with the wide historical sweep?' his friend from New York had asked him. He had no answer, no solution. If history was synecdoche, happiness, perhaps, was metaphor.) Each time he tried to complete the story, the images that beset him were of unacknowledged mourning, how he hadn't wept for his dead and even those friends and lovers he'd lost through circumstance and mistakes.

He was sitting at his desk by the window, trying to see if he could assemble the fragments of 'Happiness' into a mosaic, experimenting in a desultory way with line breaks, mostly looking out at a mauve sky. (In a fortnight the clocks would go back; a pall of darkness would come down early on the city and on him.) The phone rang: Maryam, making an unexpected call. She had a sheaf of translations someone had made of her work into French. She wondered whether he had an hour or two. They could meet in a café by a bookshop, in which they often sat and smoked and showed each other stories and poems. His eyes felt heavy with sleep, but the anticipation of seeing Maryam lifted his drooping eyelids. (He loved the ability she displayed, in her poetry, to make the cerebral sensuous and the tactile intellectual; she also understood the ellipses, gaps and frustrations that made all emotional entanglements so maddening. In spite of occasional distances and differences, their tender and almost unconditional mutual affection, very like the love of siblings, had kept them close for more than a decade.)

Outside the window the leaves were still dense on the trees, but their colours were turning. It occurred to him then that in trying to keep out the cold he'd been armouring himself too long with the heaviness of leather. He decided to leave his flat in the thin short-sleeved blue linen shirt he'd put on after his shower.

He stepped out. Rain was forming little puddles on the pavement and the air was biting. But the rain was very fine and the cool air on his bare arms calmed him. The sky was purple, distant. Once the sky touched me. I can't remember where or when that was. But if it touched me once, it might even touch me again.

Two years ago he had gone with Maryam to spend some days in a seaside town in Dorset, sharing with her the silence and calm of those who have to learn to live with sadness. (Murad was mourning for a friend who had been hit by a car as she crossed the road to the park; she had gone, after hovering between life and death for a week, at the age of twenty-seven, leaving many poems and stories unpublished. Maryam, perhaps, though she said little about her

burden, was thinking of her son who'd been ill for two years.)
They'd found themselves by a narrow river, flanked on one shore
by a street lined with cafés and antique shops and on the other
by yellow, blue and pink houses with touches and trimmings of
chalky white. At one of the miniscule jetties scattered along its
banks they'd boarded a fragile boat that ferried them across the
water to a point not far from where the river met the sea. They'd
walked a while along the esplanade and found a spot where they
stopped, leaning their elbows on a convenient iron railing above
a sheer drop to the sea. They lit cigarettes and looked at the
waves in high tide. On the beach below, bands of children and
teenagers, spurred by some local competition, were attempting
to build life-sized sculptures of castles, horses and other fantastic
shapes, embellished with bits of broken glass, shiny foil and scraps
of metal. Then the clouds parted. The greyish sea changed colour
and was full of light, as bright as a field of giant yellow sunflowers.
The yellow-streaked sky was very close. Happiness and despair
partake of each other: are the interplay of leaf and shadow, sun
and its reflection in water, rain on earth and rock. He stood there
with Maryam, not talking. After a while – not short, not long
– they walked on, in wordless unison.

The Lark

'Strawberries!'

'Hmmm. Strawberries. From my garden.'

'Lovely! Mmmm!'

'Hmmm. Yes. Strawberries. Picked them myself.'

'Mmmmm. Lovely. Strawberries.'

Lady Ann handed over the basket to Mrs Bridge, took off her hat and gloves, paused for a moment, looked around the room and intoned: 'Where's the Black Prince, then?'

And when no one responded she said quite plaintively, 'Weren't you going to have your Black Prince for tea?'

Mrs Bridge moved forward. 'Do meet Mr Hassan Khan, Ann. He's from India. He's been studying with Oliver at Magdalen. He's come to visit ...'

But Lady Ann wasn't to be deterred. 'Oh, the Prince!' She curtsied; Hassan bowed slightly. 'But you're terribly pale for an Indian, Your Royal Highness. I'd have taken you for a Frenchman ...'

Oliver stepped in. 'Hassan doesn't like to be called a prince, Aunt Ann. His title is Nawabzada. He says his family would be sitting in the Lords here.'

Hassan, only faintly amused at Lady Ann's anticipation of an encounter with a swarthy turbanned exotic as a source of teatime entertainment, was still wondering about the strawberry ritual. So quaint. Was there some hidden code in the women's words that he couldn't decipher?

It was Lucy who answered his question the next morning, as they wheeled their bicycles down the hill. 'Mmm. First fruits of the season, you know. Strawberries. Very special.'

Hassan said, 'If someone had brought one of my aunts a gift of fruit, let's say mangoes, there would have been a discussion about its colour, its flavour, its season and the quality of rain and soil it needs, the best time of day to eat it ...'

'Yes. Well.'

'I think old Ann was a bit disappointed with you, young man. Far too pale and ordinary looking, you are, and then your clothes ... at least you could have worn your tall grey woolly hat, if you don't know how to do a turban.'

(They'd considered the possibility of Hassan wrapping a green paisley scarf of Lucy's around his head, turban-style, to oblige the old lady. But a prank had misfired last year when Hassan had been persuaded by classmates to dress up in improvised regalia for a costume party; his picture was published in the papers, which mentioned emerald necklaces, diamond buttons and ruby turban ornaments; his guardian sent it to his father, and he was reprimanded for boasting: he'd blamed Oliver for taking it all too far.)

They were walking to the sea, and it was a fair way. After an hour's hike downhill, they went up a steep incline to a wooden fence and a turnstile, through a poppy-starred field of billowing wheat. They found a dust track. Above their heads a lark soared, swooped and sang a coloratura solo. When they stopped, the lark, too, would stop, coming down to the earth to hop along a few yards in front of them. She'd sing some notes in a colloquial, less bravura register, and when she was sure they were following her, she'd rise in the air again.

'Larks make their nests in the fields,' Lucy said.

'I don't understand just why you've chosen this time to leave.' Oliver was back on his favoured topic of the day. 'What if the Krauts start bombing before you reach Suez? Or sink your ship? And that's not the greatest worry. What if you can't get out of India once you're there? It's our final year, you know ...'

Hassan was finding it harder and harder not to tell him the truth.

'And you're never going to be back in time for the start of term ...'

'I left home four years ago, and I've only been back once. I've lived in Oxford since I was sixteen, spending my holidays with my guardian or in London with that ghastly landlady in Baker Street. I'd really like a spell at home.'

The lark, trilling and pirouetting in the air, had led them to the edge of the cliff, and they could see the sea stretching out below them, turbulent, capped with white. It wasn't a view one would expect at the end of a field. Hassan breathed in the salt air and closed his eyes. When he opened them, the lark was a tiny speck high above their heads. Rewarded by the knowledge that she'd led them away from her nest and her progeny, she'd abdicated her guide's role without a final backward glance.

'Look! Count them! There are only six Marys and there should be seven,' Lucy said, pointing to the row of whitish cliffs just beyond them.

'We're standing on the seventh Mary, silly.' Oliver was, as usual, impatient with his younger sister.

'How do you know it's the seventh and not the first? One, two, three, four ...'

'O do shut up.'

Hand on her eyes, Lucy turned and ran like a little goat down the narrow path that led to the sea.

'Now look what you've done. You've made her cry.' Hassan left his friend and made his way down the path, less surefooted than Lucy as he ran in his light shoes, dislodging little shoals of pebbles.

The narrow strip of beach at the bottom of the cliff path was littered with molluscs and shells. Lucy was squatting by the edge of the water, squinting into the distance. Hassan knelt beside her; for a moment, he thought of putting a hand on one forlorn shoulder, but didn't. Instead, he peered at her profile, which was half hidden under the brim of the large hat she wore to protect her pale complexion.

'I'm not crying, silly. Something in my eye,' she said, rubbing one eyelid with the knuckles of her right hand. She took off her hat and shook out her wavy red hair. 'One of those ships will take you all the way to India,' she added after a silent while. 'Across the Channel to France, then to the Mediterranean and Africa, then to the ocean … which one? The Atlantic?'

'The Indian Ocean. Karachi, where I'll disembark, is on the Arabian Sea.'

'Would I like India, do you think? Will it be too, too hot for me? How many wives does your Papa the Maharaja have? Would I make a nice Maharani?'

'I'm sure you'd love India for a few weeks. We'd take you to all the right places. Then you'll complain about the weather and the food and probably get ill. And my father has only one wife. I've told you that. She's my stepmother, I told you that too, and she's American. My mother died ten years ago. Most of us don't marry more than once.'

'What about you? Didn't you marry when you were ten?'

Hassan sighed. 'No.'

The sky was clouding over. Close up, the water was purplish:

the colour of seaweed?

'But Oliver said ...'

'Here's my lovely sister angling for a marriage proposal, and you really ought to tell her you're spoken for ...' They hadn't noticed Oliver creep up on them. 'He carries a picture of a girl in his wallet and won't show it to anyone; he writes to her every week, and she answers in this funny script, upside down and back to front ... so I thought he must have been married all his life.'

'I'M NOT MARRIED.'

'But now you're leaving us. When will you come back? Will you invite us to India for your wedding celebration?'

So Lucy knew instinctively what he hadn't told Oliver.

(Oliver was agitated about Hassan's attitude to the war. Long ago, when they'd been talking about the conflict in Spain, Oliver had said he'd have gone to fight if he hadn't been so young. On which side? Hassan had wanted to know. For the king, Oliver said. And which side was the king on? Hassan asked, before launching into a diatribe about Franco and the rights and wrongs of Spain's political situation. And yesterday, on their way to Oliver's family home, they'd argued again, this time about the war to come. We should lay down our lives for king and country, Oliver claimed. But what about the pacifists and the republicans, Hassan rejoindered. You're a disloyal subject of the British Empire, Oliver said. I come from a Native State, Hassan replied, I'm not a British subject. And what am I to Hitler? Oliver choked, spluttered, coughed. Such a strong reaction? Hassan wanted to slap his friend's back, but instead he said, I'm sorry. It's miasma, Oliver muttered among coughs and groans. Hassan stood there in consternation. Miasma? What did that have to do with war or loyalty?)

'What time's your boat?'

'I'll take the 5.40 from Folkestone.'

'I'll sit here a while, maybe bathe or just watch the sea. No, don't shake my hand or say goodbye, I can't bear goodbyes, I start sniffling. Even if I'm only saying farewell to my terrier for three days.'

How volatile they were, Oliver and Lucy and all their relatives, their humour changing from moment to moment, tears and laughter and raised voices all in the space of twenty minutes. (Hassan and Oliver had met at the start of their second year, beginning as rivals in the debating society and now Hassan felt he wouldn't have known how to cope with life at Oxford without his older friend, who took him boating and riding and hiking on Saturdays. And holidays – the few days he'd spend with them in the country were enough for him, but he'd find himself counting the days in London before he could leave for Kent. And though he usually felt a degree of relief when he reclaimed his solitude after sharing his friend's bedroom and tolerating his abominable habits – Oliver wiped his feet and then his face on the same towel, and blew his nose loudly in lavatory paper – he'd miss the noisy, warmhearted Bridges, their eccentric meals and the good, plain roasts that sometimes appeared on their table, their arguments and their dissensions, their untended garden, their many dogs, the seaside not far from their house, little Lucy's candid affection.)

'Do you remember the rabbit stew? And those eels?' Guessing that Hassan was reminiscing, Oliver slapped his back as they climbed up the steep path. 'Ha, ha, ha. Mother served them up for Sunday supper and you sat down at table and you saw those big, slimy slices wobbling in their dish and you went white – you thought we were eating snake! Poor Mother knew she'd made yet another faux pas. She said, O dear, is it another of the things Mohammedans are forbidden to eat? And you had to make do with stale bread and carrots and peas! And the time you drank a toast in water? And remember the first time you saw the wash basin in my room and you didn't know how to wash in it or to use your flannel? You funny old foreigner. Ha, ha.'

They took a turn that didn't lead them through wheatfields and poppies. This was another landscape altogether, denser, greener. To their right were some stones that, closer up, turned out to be ruins in a half-standing enclosure; possibly the ancient ruins of a temple or a graveyard. It had started to rain slightly, a fine cold rain. As they passed the walls of the enclosure, they saw a flock of sheep; but unlike the whitish-yellow sheep you usually found in these parts, these sheep were silvery blue. They were converging on one of their number that seemed to be wounded or ill, sniffing and stroking her, in turn.

It was raining harder now, and they tacitly decided to run to the gate they could see in the distance. When they reached it Oliver was badly out of breath again; his freckles stood out against a very white skin which made his red hair look redder. Hassan now worked out what Oliver's miasma was. Oliver couldn't run for long, or bear contact with pollen, nettles, cat's fur, grass and a host of other things: his reactions to nature's inimical realities – he sneezed, had coughing fits, choked, became breathless, shed copious tears – could be quite terrifying.

'Time to leave for the station as soon as we get home and you've got your bags,' Oliver said. 'Still can't understand why you have to lug all your stuff across the ocean. You're only going for ten weeks, for Christ's sake. Leave some of it with me.'

The night before, while Oliver carefully labelled all his suitcases 'Prince Hassan' ('Titles go down well on ships'), Hassan had taken off his heavy Swiss watch to give to his friend, who had so often admired it. But Oliver had shown no pleasure, taking it reluctantly with a muttered 'You shouldn't,' almost as if to avoid the embarrassment of refusal. 'Take care of your asthma,' Hassan had said.

And now there was nothing more to give or say and only the guilt of a kept secret stood between them. Hassan wasn't going to tell Oliver that he was leaving England for ever, or at least till the Europeans' war was over; he was leaving his studies at Magdalen unfinished; his father was going to keep him in the relative safety of India while the war went on; Hassan had a place at Lahore

University, where he would join in the third year and wouldn't even lose any academic time.

One day, though, I might come back. To see Lucy and Oliver and Mrs Bridge. When the bloody war's over.

There's something still left to tell Oliver, though, he thought as they drove to the station. My father showed me some pictures in Paris last year. I was nineteen and he thought it was time for me to think of marriage. All the pictures were pretty, but there was one of a girl who looked as if she didn't want to be photographed tall, slim, right elbow resting on a column, left hand grazing the folds of her clothes. Sleek, silky hair and a side parting. Perfect features and deep, dark eyes that seemed to look out at me. This one, I said. She's the one for me. She comes from one of the best families, my father said. They've ruled in the same state for eight hundred years and the British never even got there. They even have their own mint and their own stamps. They may have no time for us, our family has been in India only three hundred years, though we've had the best of things in recent times. I don't want to look at any one else, I told him. I want to be with her. Later I saw her, at a wedding. She knew someone was looking at her and she stalked off. Someone told me she sang beautifully, too. I love beautiful singing. I knew I wanted to spend the rest of my life with her. Soon after that her family formally accepted our proposal. I like to think she chose me, I heard she'd kept a lot of people waiting and then it was me she finally accepted. We'll marry when I graduate. My people travelled to her town with gifts and a ring, a cabochon ruby surrounded by diamonds. I chose that, and another gift for her, too: monogrammed writing paper from Tiffany's, with her own variation on our family crest in pale blue and silver. I stole the picture: I had it copied and tinted, and I carry it with me. Always.

But he didn't even have time to start his story. They'd nearly reached the port of departure. As they turned a corner, a field of silver caught his eye. For the second time that day, neat and very close, spread out just to his right as smooth as a mirror in the sun, the sea was waiting for him. The sea that would take him home.

A Note on the Author

Aamer Hussein was born in 1955 in Karachi, Pakistan. He grew up in Karachi and spent most summers in India. He studied in South India for two years before moving to London in 1970. He read Persian, Urdu and History at SOAS, and later taught Urdu for many years at the SOAS Language Centre. He has since lectured in the English Department at Queen Mary College (London), and is currently associated with the MA programme in National and International Literatures at the School of Advanced Study's Institute of English Studies (Senate House). He has also held writing fellowships at the University of Southampton and at Imperial College. His first collection of stories, *Mirror to the Sun*, was published in 1993. Since then, he has published two other collections – *This Other Salt* (1999) and *Turquoise* (2002). He has also edited a volume of stories by Pakistani women, *Kahani*. He was made a Fellow of the Royal Society of Literature in 2004. He reviews regularly for *The Independent*, and writes occasional essays for *Tehelka* (Delhi). He continues to live in London, and spends most winter vacations in Asia.